The Alpha's Biker-Kissed Omega

By

Lorelei M. Hart

Editor Wizards in Publishing

Cover design by Fantasia Frog Designs

Published by Decadent Publishing LLC

I've been giving Axel not so subtle hints for months to no avail. He comes in once a week for a shave and takes a piece of my heart with him every time he goes. The late night barber shop here at Principal Ink feels more like home than the crowded apartment I share with several roommates.

I know Brandon wants me as much as I want him, but there's a secret I've kept from the people at the shop and exposing my secret might burst the bubble I've created. He might not want me after I reveal what I've been hiding.

One night, a box shows up at principal ink, a box that will change our lives forever. Axel won't have a choice but to come clean but will Brandon ever be able to trust him again?

The Alpha-Kissed Series by Lorelei M. Hart

The Alpha's Autumn-Kissed Omega

The Alpha's Candy-Kissed Omega

The Alpha's Cranberry-Kissed Omega

The Alpha's Santa-Kissed Omega

The Alpha's Ginger-Kissed Omega

The Alpha's Lifeguard-Kissed Omega

The Alpha's Principal-Kissed Omega

The Alpha's Biker-Kissed Omega

Coming Soon!

The Alpha's Soda-Kissed Omega

The Alpha's Preacher-Kissed Omega

Chapter One

Axel

The knot at my throat seemed to cut off my breath...

After a long week of dealing with the corporate client from hell, nothing felt better than parking the BMW the firm assigned me in my high-rise garage and emerging again on my Harley. I'd shed my bespoke suit like the snakeskin I considered it and donned jeans worn thin by use, black boots, a white T-shirt, and my leather jacket.

The weekend's uniform.

Oh, and the legally required helmet.

The uniform of the weekend. Late enough the traffic heading to the suburbs had thinned to almost nothing, the reward for sticking around the office until I'd dealt with enough work to leave for Saturday and Sunday.

Once past the city limits, the open road beckoned and I opened up the bike, risking a ticket, but I didn't care. If I didn't let off steam, I'd lose my mind. And the risk was low, since the patrolman on the Friday night beat out here was another patron of the social club I frequented. As long as I didn't push it too far, Ted would probably turn his head. Ted was one of the few at the club who knew more about me than what kind of bike I rode. And since I knew a few things about his life...we just kept each other's secrets.

The spring evening was cool enough to want the jacket, but laden with the scents of flowers bursting into bloom. Nothing like the choking exhaust of town. I never rode my bike there, unless it was on my way to or from Roseville.

My true home.

Usually I'd stop by the cottage, have a beer, sit for a while in the peace and quiet, but usually I managed to get away before ten o'clock. Tonight, I steered right up to the front of Principal Ink and parked in the row of others. Machines gleaming under the neon sign, polished and babied by owners who shared my passion for the roaring engines and shiny chrome. I dismounted and stowed the helmet in my saddlebag before stretching my back and inhaling a deep breath of the particular perfume that infused this place.

Ink, bay rum, exhaust, chrome polish...and leather. Primarily anyway.

"Axel, I thought you might not make it tonight!" One of the regular guys was just swinging a leg over his Indian, a classic I always admired even though I'd somehow never learned the owner's name. But he knew mine, so I made a mental note to learn it.

"Yeah, work kept me late. Busy in there?" I jerked a thumb in the direction of the social lounge tucked between the tatt shop and the barber's.

"Kinda. A bunch of the guys are out of town on that tour, but still enough to get up a pool game." His bike roared, a belch of smoke from the pipes. "I won't be in tomorrow—gotta find the problem in Betsy before it gets serious."

"Sure. Good luck." I watched him ride off down the street, another belch of smoke halfway down. An old beauty like that required an owner with plenty of time to tinker. Even having stolen back most of my weekends after achieving partnership status, I didn't have that much time. Shams, though...as he disappeared into the night, I turned with a sigh and headed inside.

Someday I'd get my hands on the bike of my dreams. Probably after I retired.

Inside the building, I waved to Ranger who was bent over an arm, filling in a sleeve, looked like. He nodded and I continued on, passing the small room usually occupied by the piercer, when they had one on staff. The most recent occupant had taken a job in Alaska, leaving them short-staffed.

Heading through the lounge area, I noticed only a dozen or so guys playing pool and sitting around shooting the breeze. Three by the electronic dartboard. Must be a big group on that tour. I wished I'd been able to go, but until yesterday I hadn't even been sure I'd be able to get away. My job paid well and allowed me to keep my dads in the senior community, playing golf and telling lies about their fishing, but sometimes it was too big a pain in the—

"Axel." I'd been so lost in thought I hadn't heard the door on the other side of the lounge open, but when I looked up, there he stood. All five-foot-eleven of him. He wore his white barber jacket with jeans I knew from past experience were skin-tight and showed off the nicest bubble butt in town. "It's good to see you. How was your week?"

"It sucked. As always." And the last of the tension slipped away. "How was yours?"

He grinned, wrinkling his freckled nose and looking far younger than the twenty-six I knew he was. "Great. I have lots of stories. Want to hear?"

4

Like all hair professionals, Brandon heard it all. And, lucky me, I was the one he liked to share all the gossip with. It helped me feel more like a local and less like a weekender. "You know I do. Got coffee on?"

"Fresh pot. Come sit in my chair."

Chapter Two

Brandon

The closest I could get to having Axel on a date was getting him to sit in my chair. I looked around the shop to make sure no one was watching as I wrapped the ink-black cape around his broad shoulders. The time I spent with him felt so intimate, at least, on my end.

Axel had never made a move, and I'd given him plenty of opportunities to do so.

He liked his beard long, but kempt. I liked to give him the old-school treatment. Hot cloth, brushed on shaving cream, and a straight razor to get his shave as close as possible. I rolled my eyes at myself. If I was a smart man, I would give him a not-so-good shave so he would come back over and over.

I bet a man like him did a lot of coming over and over.

Fuck. I needed to calm the hell down or else everyone would know in an instant how I felt about Axel from the tent in my pants.

While I mixed up the shaving cream, he took a few

sips of his coffee, and our eyes met in the mirror.

"So what story do you want to hear? The guy who came in for a Betty Boop tattoo, or the one who came in with a design spelled incorrectly?"

He chuckled, and his gaze never left mine. "Let's do both, but misspelling first."

"That was last night about midnight. He came in, white as a sheet, and said he'd drawn the damned thing himself. Armison was in here checking on some things while he's still on leave with the baby and broke out in laughter when he leaned over Mike's shoulder to look at it. Of course, the dude was offended—it was his art. But Armison, you know him, ripped the damned thing in half, saying that his former principal self wouldn't allow misspellings in his shop."

I brushed some shaving cream onto his cheeks and neck, loving the way every stroke almost let me touch his skin. The act was like a massage.

"Well what happened then?"

I smiled down at him, reaching to let the chair lean back. His face was at my waist, and I'd conjured up more than one fantasy about him simply turning his head and giving me the sexual relief I needed with his mouth.

Empty shop, of course.

8

I moved to the other side to sidetrack my thoughts.

"He ended up getting a skull. Of all things, a skull. No words. Nothing else. And he cried during the whole thing. Armison broke his damned heart."

He chuckled for a bit and then sobered when I took out the razor. I didn't think, or I hoped he wasn't scared of me but wanted to keep still to help me.

I held the metal in the air, telling him without words that I was about to begin. "Do you have any tats, Brandon?"

Gods above, he stirred my baser passions with my name coming out of his luscious mouth.

"I have some. Small ones. None that are misspelled," I murmured, trying and failing to bring some comedy into the equation before I mounted him like he did his motorcycle right there in front of paying customers and the world.

He was asking about me this time. He hadn't done that before.

He grunted. Not the answer I wanted to hear, but then again, I'd begun shaving him, so he'd chosen not to mess me up.

I paid attention to each stroke of metal against his smooth skin. Most customers closed their eyes or even held up their phones and scrolled while I shaved them or did their hair, but not Axel. He looked at my face through the entire process. My groin pushed against his side as I reached and postured myself for a better angle to get everything just right. I knew he could feel my hardness as there was only that thin cape and his T-shirt between us.

I chanced a look into his eyes. They were trained on me and, for those twenty or so minutes while I did my job, it was only me and him in the world—in the fucking universe.

But still, he never asked me out.

What was holding him back?

A loud guffaw and some high-fiving broke my thought process, and I quickly finished up his neck. I got another towel and cleaned him up, taking my time.

If he was mine and I was his, I would shave him every day in our bathroom, not even the cape or clothes between us.

Gods, I had to stop daydreaming and night dreaming and anything-else dreaming about him.

If he wanted me, he would've said so.

He tipped me well and then went to the other side of the business for a round of pool with his friends. I had no more customers, so I spent the time cleaning my tools and restocking things for the next day. The weekends were busy and exhausting, but they brought in the most tips.

Most of them filed out about midnight, but Axel and a few others lingered.

I wiped down my chair one last time and clicked off the light at my station when I heard a car screech into the parking lot. Someone got out and with a package in their hand, walked to the front door, dropped it, and then peeled out as fast as they had come in.

"What the hell was that?" I asked no one in particular. "Who drops packages this late at night?"

Chapter Three

Axel

Time to call it a night.

No matter how long a week, and this was a long one, I always popped into Principal Ink on Friday night for at least a game of pool, some BS with the group, and a shave from Brandon. I did that to torture myself. The omega had dropped enough hints that he was interested in something beyond a barber/customer relationship, and we did always have good conversations, but I made sure it stopped there. He spent a ridiculous amount of time on me, for a weekly shave and monthly haircut, but I made sure to tip enough to cover his time. If I'd been looking for an omega, Brandon would have been it. But I lived a double life, and the fun guy who hung out at the club on the weekends was nothing like the Monday morning to Friday afternoon buttoned-down suit who followed the rules to get ahead at a big city law firm. Corporate stooge whose days were committed to one despicable client.

Once he was done neatening up the beard, one as long and full as I could get away with in my line of work, convo over. I had no more excuses to be in the barbershop, not until the next week. I couldn't lead him on, yet I also couldn't force myself to stop going in there on Friday nights. I lived for that hour. When he leaned over me, the long, thick length of him pressed against me told me how willing he'd be to spend a little private time together. The only thing that hid my matching response was the black cape he draped over my front to keep me neat and tidy.

But it was getting harder each week to keep these worlds separate. Everyone here knew I was away during the week, but somehow word had gotten around that I drove a truck. Blue-collar guy like many of those here. Sure, there were a few other professionals, but I'd never encountered them in the city, and since I wasn't especially proud of my work at the moment, and since the only other attorney, an estate lawyer with a shingle downtown, was "too good" to use my barber crush's services for his pretty hairstyle, I had neglected to correct the general opinion.

There was nothing wrong with long-distance trucking. It was an honorable profession, just not my honorable profession. Still, as I racked the balls for one last game of eight ball, I felt a little guilty. Even if I hadn't started the deceit, I'd done nothing to end it. And the guilt led to a loss of twenty bucks to the great delight of my opponent.

He clapped me on the back. "I never thought I'd beat you. Maybe you had a rough route this week." Stuffing the bill in his pocket he headed outside, calling over his shoulder as he mounted his bike. "Hey, somebody left a box out here." He gunned the engine, and soon the rumble faded into the distance.

At nearly three in the morning, the day, heck, the week, had started to weigh on me. I might not have a "route" but I did have five very long shifts of dealing with assholes behind me, and if I didn't get home soon, I'd be asleep on my feet. Most of the other guys were already gone, Fridays not running as late as Saturdays, since almost everyone had worked all day before coming to the club.

Stretching, I reached for my jacket, just as Brandon appeared in the doorway between the barbershop and the club. "Did anyone grab that package?"

"Huh?" I suppressed my delight at seeing him again. "No, I guess not. Someone just said there's a box out there. I wonder what it is?"

Brandon shrugged. "I don't know, but curious minds want to know. Armison has already gone home, so I guess that leaves me in charge. I'll get it."

"Now I'm curious. Maybe it's a million dollars."

"More likely an Amazon delivery that was due by nine tonight."

I chuckled and followed him, slipping my arms into my jacket as I did. Brandon wasn't wearing a barber's coat tonight, as I'd kind of noticed when he was shaving me. His T-shirt outlined every bit of toned muscle this omega had to offer, and as we stepped outside, I focused on the twin globes of his ass. If I had a type...he was it.

"I think it's over here somewhere," he muttered. "Yeah, here it is and...holy shit." He froze, half bent over, and I came to his side to see what elicited such a reaction.

"Holy shit," I echoed.

"I already said that." And he had. But who wouldn't, when faced with the contents of that cardboard box. It wasn't an Amazon delivery unless they'd changed their terms of service. Because in that box, nestled in a blue blanket, one chubby fist stuffed in his mouth, was a baby.

"It's a baby," Brandon breathed. "Why is there a baby here?"

"I don't have a clue," I told him, my brain flashing to all kinds of reasons there might be a baby. "But we can't leave him out here in the cold."

Chapter Four

Brandon

The first idiotic thought in my head was whether or not Amazon was delivering babies nowadays.

That was how shocked I was to see a baby in a box.

But as the babe began to wail, probably somehow knowing he'd just been abandoned by his parents. I picked him up out of the box and rushed him inside. We didn't really have baby blankets just lying around the tattoo shop, so I grabbed one of the clean towels from the back and wrapped him in it as tightly as I could. I'd seen once where babies like to be wrapped up tightly, like they were in the womb.

"He doesn't look very old," Axel said. He had followed me into the back along with the stares of everyone in the place. It wasn't every day that we got a baby dropped at our door.

"He?" I asked him, looking up to see his eyes still bulging.

"He's got a blue shirt on. I just assumed."

I scoffed. "Well, the parents just dropped him at a tattoo shop in the middle of the night in a box, so I'm assuming they didn't really care about his fashion. We need to call the cops—like now."

That was my hint for Axel to call them, but the big guy was frozen.

"Axel!" I said, trying to whisper-shout as loudly as possible while rocking the babe back and forth, moving my hips like my dads did when my brothers and I when we were little.

"Oh, yeah, cops. Hold on." He walked away, dialing on his phone. He must've already known the number or something. I would've had to google the damned number.

"Hey, little one. It's okay. We're going to get you somewhere safe. Not the way you imagined it, huh?" As I rocked the babe back and forth, he or she had fallen asleep, probably simply from being so cold and then warm in my arms.

"They are on their way, but social services can't come until morning."

I gasped. "It's their job to be here now."

Axel nodded. "Yeah, but this is a small town, and social services is a county service. Not many babies abandoned in Roseville. We will have to wait."

I looked down at the babe's tiny face and perfectly rounded nose. His ginger hair was only wisps. And I kept calling it a he.

"I'm not keeping a baby in a tattoo shop, Axel."

He bit down on his bottom lip, and I almost growled. I'd dreamed about those lips for months. I would be happy to do the biting myself if he'd let me.

"Bring him to your place," he said finally.

"I-I can't. I have roommates."

His reddened face and furrowed brow said it all.

"Not mates. Roommates. I have to in order to keep a roof over my head. Barbers don't really make a lot of money, if you hadn't noticed. My roommates are messy and probably drunk off their asses about now. No way I'm bringing a babe over there. Shit, what do I do?"

He cleared his throat and toggled his gaze from me to the babe. "We can bring him back to my house."

I almost laughed. "We?"

I'd never seen Axel look anything but self-confident and assured, but this tiny creature had him looking all kinds of uncomfortable. "Yeah, we. I wouldn't know what to do with a baby, even for a few hours."

I blew out a weighted breath. "Let's wait for the cops and then decide."

Just as the words left my mouth, I heard the ding of the bell at the front door. We were in the process of closing, so it must've been the cops.

For the next half hour, I recounted the events of the baby dropping and so did every patron in the place. Finally, after three officers interviewed everyone, they were satisfied that we weren't some hoaxers or whatever else they thought.

"Social services can be reached at this number, though we have already called and left them the information to get in touch with you, Axel." I'd noticed through their asking questions that they seemed to know Axel. Maybe he'd been in trouble with the law.

"Thank you. We will be at my house if you need us."

Us. Sounded so damned good.

"Come on. Do you need to grab anything?" he asked, taking my elbow with his hand.

"If you can get my gear bag, that would be great. You came on your bike?"

He cursed under his breath.

"That's fine. We can take my car."

He grabbed my bag, and I handed over the keys.

22

We didn't have a car seat, so I got into the back and put my seat belt on. "Go slow. It's freaking me out not to have a car seat."

Axel nodded and met my eyes in the rearview mirror.

When he stopped at a drugstore, I nearly freaked out. "What are you doing?"

He shrugged and moved to get out. "Diapers, bottles, formula. Otherwise, the next few hours will be hell for all three of us."

Well, he wasn't wrong.

And Axel said he knew nothing about babies.

In minutes, he was back, and we drove into a gated neighborhood that made me drool. Huge two-story houses that all seemed to look the same and boasted high-end cars in every driveway.

Damn, I guess truck drivers really did make bank.

"This is me," he said and drove into one of the few houses that looked a little different from the others. His wasn't painted the plain khaki. Instead, it was a rust color with beautiful dark wood trim, at least from what I could see in my pitiful headlights.

I took my time getting out of the car and he escorted us, bags in hand, to the front door. He pushed a few numbers into the electronic lock, and inside we went.

I gasped a little too loudly.

"What?" he asked, trying to see what I did.

"This place is amazing."

Then the baby began to wail.

Chapter Five

Axel

The cottage? Amazing? I tried to see it through Brandon's eyes. It was a nice place, well maintained, and certainly bigger than some of the homes in Roseville, but not fancy in any way. I had filled it with comfortable overstuffed furniture, and the big eat-in kitchen had been one of the selling points when I bought it. Not that I cooked much, and since I did my socializing at the club, I never had anyone at the gleaming wood table to share dinner with. Or breakfast.

If I had invited any of the guys, they'd have known I wasn't a truck driver. I recognized that now. And also, that the jig would be up by the time social services showed up for the baby in the morning.

Brandon stood inside the door, holding the little one in his arms and looking around as if he'd never seen a house before. Which brought it home even more how different my lifestyle was compared to a lot of the people I hung out with every weekend. I didn't keep any of my suits here, but a glance in my closet would show him that even my casual clothes were designer label. Sure, my leathers were nice, but a lot of the guys spent their spare change on the best riding stuff. The difference was, all of my clothes were expensive.

Hell, I had a personal shopper who bought them, to save me the time. During the week, in order to have the weekends mostly free, I barely took time to sleep. Or eat. Which left me starving on the weekends, even if most of my meals were takeout.

A wail from the wrapped-up infant in Brandon's arms startled me. I wasn't the only one hungry. He shifted the baby to his shoulder and patted the little back. "Can you make a bottle for him? I think you need to sterilize it first."

Honestly...I had no idea. But what I did have was access to the Internet. I ducked into my office...the one that would show Brandon what I did for a living if he ever saw it, and grabbed my tablet from the table by the sofa. I locked the door behind me, wanting the omega to learn the truth from me rather than the shelves of law books lining my office. It was the single room not country casual. Dark wood, maroon leather...heavy drapes. A wide-screen monitor mounted on the wall for meetings I could not manage to avoid. Yeah. A complete giveaway.

"Axel?" The omega sounded more distressed than the baby. "What's taking so long?"

"I'm coming!" I assured him, bustling back into the living room. "Let's go in the kitchen and we'll look up how to feed a newborn without making him sick."

"Okay." He followed me, bouncing the baby in his arms. "Hang in there, little guy. It's gonna be okay." Plopping down at the table, he took a sniff. "I think we have more than just a hungry little person here."

The scent wafted toward me where I stood at the counter, clicking away at the tablet. I winced. "Ever changed a diaper?"

"Me? No. I was the baby in the family. Everyone changed my diapers."

"And I was an only child, didn't even have cousins. I've only seen diapers on TV." I searched YouTube for diaper-changing advice. The first one was not at all what I was looking for and I quickly clicked on to the next. I had no objection to what adults liked to do together, it just wasn't my thing. Especially not right now.

"Axel? Are you having any luck?" His voice held a tinge of desperation. "I'm going to faint."

I looked up from the screen and stared at him. "Faint?"

His eyes watered. "From the smell. How can such a cute little thing make so much noise and such noxious fumes?"

"Okay. Don't panic." I clicked again. "Here is a video put up by one of the diaper companies. They should know how to do it, right?"

"I...yes." He lifted the soggy, stinky baby. "Where do we do it?"

Good question. I eyed the table, the counter, the bench seat by the window... "Let me get a towel." I ducked out and came back with a bath sheet, which I laid over the window seat, doubled up. "I hope this is good enough." Even though it was "casual comfortable," I didn't really want the upholstery to smell like...well whatever the baby did right now.

Together we went to work, propping the tablet on the windowsill so we could pause and start the video as we went along. And everything went pretty well...at first. We removed the diaper and cleaned his bottom. Turned out we should have bought something called wipes, but wet washcloths did the trick. I'd probably throw them away after.

Then it happened. Just as the nice smiling lady on the screen told us to be sure to cover a boy baby's little boy parts, we found out why.

Chapter Six

Brandon

"Well, we know he's not dehydrated," I said and shrugged. It wasn't a big deal for me. With four brothers, I'd seen it all. My parents had both gotten peed on, and we boys potty trained by leaving the back door open and 'watering the plants'. It worked for us. Axel looked completely shocked like he didn't know our parts did that. "Hey, can you hold him a minute? I need to go wash my face."

"Oh, um, that's not a good idea," he said, waving his hands frantically in front of him.

"Yes, it is. I'm not going to spend the rest of the night covered in pee. Come here." I fastened the diaper, wrapped the babe up in the towel, and held him out to Axel. "Sit down in that chair."

He did as I asked, white as a damned sheet. It was a baby, not a tiny vampire. I've never seen someone so scared.

"Hold his head," I said and put the babe down in his arms.

"Why? Does it come off?" he asked, but was

already caught up in the cherub face of the cooing babe. "Go. Hurry up before I break him."

I rolled my eyes and rushed to the bathroom, except I didn't know where it was so I had to open and shut a couple of doors before finding it.

"Damn," I whispered as I entered the bathroom. The place had a full glass shower with eight thousand showerheads and one of those modern sinks seen only on commercials.

I pulled the lever on the metal faucet and watched as the water swirled into the bowl on top of the counter. Fancy.

Two minutes later, I walked back into Axel's living room and covered my mouth at the scene. The baby boy was sound asleep while Axel cradled him in two large hands and swayed him back and forth. He was like a human baby hammock.

He could rock me to sleep every night like that.

"What's going to happen to him," he murmured and looked up at me with those large eyes.

"I guess social services will place him somewhere."

"He deserves better," he said so softly I almost didn't catch the sentence.

I sat in the chair next to him and watched in awe the man who seconds ago didn't want to hold him at all

32

do a stellar job of handling the little one. The baby's hands were folded over his chest looking downright angelic.

Who would ever throw a baby away?

Someone desperate, I supposed.

"Do you want me to take him?" I asked.

"No, I think I'm good. Can I..." He never finished his question. Instead, he maneuvered the babe so that it was lying on his chest and leaned back.

"Go ahead and get some sleep. He's snug as can be on your chest. They like the sound of your heartbeat."

He nodded and before long his breaths slowed, became more even.

I took the chance to really look at the alpha as he slept. Seeing him with a babe propped on his chest and sleeping did things to me. Not that every breath he took didn't absolutely turn me on, but this was a view of my fantasy future with the burly man.

Damn, I wanted him so badly.

"I can't sleep with you staring at me." He cocked one eye open and smiled. "Get some sleep. You worked hard last night."

I worked hard, all right. I worked on him with a hard-on was more like it.

"Okay." I lay back against his gray oversized chair

and took in the scent of his place, warm and comforting around me.

Before long, I felt sleep overtake me.

I woke sometime later to Axel touching my leg. "Hey, I think he's hungry again."

Poor babe, who knows if he had been fed well. "Can you make a bottle? I'll change him."

I changed him in no time and went to the kitchen. I took the bottle from Axel and went back to the living room to sit and feed the babe who was now unruly from hunger.

"You mind if I go take a shower? I smell like smoke and, well, the tat shop."

I shrugged. "It's your house, Axel. I'm fine with this guy. Take your time." I said the words, but mentally I was screaming no. I didn't want to torture myself any more. I was in his home, surrounded by his scents. If that wasn't enough, now I had to know that he was naked, in the shower, letting his hands skim over his body, soapy and hot.

Fuck. I needed to get over this guy. I'd tried. Gods help me, I'd tried, but every time I seemed to be getting ahead, he'd walk into the shop like he owned me and knew it.

I didn't think I'd ever get over him.

I focused on the baby instead of my naughty thoughts. He gulped down the four ounces of formula in no time, and I put him over my shoulder for a burp. He squirmed and then let out one for the books before looking droopy eyed again.

Sweet little love. I wished he were mine.

"Sorry I took so long. And I realized in the shower that I've been a crappy host. Can I get you something to drink? Coffee? Tea? Are you hungry?"

I felt my face redden at him thinking about me while he was in the shower, even if it was about something silly as being a good host.

"I'm actually really hungry. I usually eat when I get off."

That's when I looked up from the babe and got an eyeful that would stay in my spank book for a lifetime. Axel had a towel around his neck and navy pajama pants slung low on his hips, revealing a beautiful V and all the veins an omega wants to see on his alpha.

The man loved to torture me.

"Bacon and eggs okay? Or do you want dinner?"

I chuckled and forced my eyes to the baby to keep from tackling him right there where he stood. "Anything is fine. I'm not picky. Thank you."

He nodded and walked away and then I looked up

on purpose.

Gods alive, the man had a million-dollar ass.

Chapter Seven

Axel

Bacon and eggs were the appropriate thing, I thought, and I flipped the strips and stirred the soft-scrambled eggs. The sun was rising outside the window, and another day dawning. So, yeah, breakfast. I was just setting everything on the table when my cell rang.

"Hello?" It was so early, it was either a work emergency—which I so did not need now—or something related to the baby.

"Axel, that you?"

"Yeah…" I still didn't know who I was talking to.

"It's Ted. I heard about your foundling. Is everything going okay?"

"Oh, hey, Ted. I guess word travels fast. Everything is fine. We're just waiting for the social worker to come take the little guy, although I'm already pretty attached. It's lucky we won't have him long."

"About that." A long pause. "Seems the single social worker in town is not in town. She's on a cruise and can't be reached. I was having coffee with the police chief this morning and he wasn't sure what to do, so I told him you'd probably be able to handle things over the weekend. I hope that's okay?"

My fingertips went numb. "What? I'm not a foster parent, I'm...well you know what I am. Why would he assume I was a good choice? Oh shit, you told him things, didn't you?" And the chief was someone who came by the club from time to time.

"I did. I'm sorry, but he was talking about sending the kid out of town and I just couldn't stand that idea."

"He'll tell everyone at the club." And Brandon would know. He wasn't a fan of white-collar types, lawyers especially, for some reason.

"Think of the baby, Axel." His voice was low and urgent. "Do you want him in that orphanage two towns over? Without even a chance of finding out how he ended up at the club?

Shit. "You're making me feel ashamed."

"Good, then maybe you won't be so mad at me for outing you." He chuckled. "I don't know why you ever hid it. It's an honorable profession."

"Then you won't mind if I share your little secrets?" Not that I would.

He let out a big sigh. "If you have to. I'll

38

understand."

"Shit, dude. I wouldn't do that. I'm not a loose-lips type like some I know."

"Okay, but will you keep the baby until Monday morning? The social worker is expected back then."

I considered my Monday schedule. I could probably shift things around for a few hours.

"Think about the baby's welfare, Axel."

"I am. I have no experience at all with babies, Ted." I glanced over my shoulder at the table where Brandon was watching me. "However...can you hang on one second?"

"Sure."

I cupped my hand over the phone. "Brandon, will you stay here for the rest of the weekend with me?"

His jaw dropped. "Here? With you?" And I inwardly cursed.

"Ted the patrolman has asked me to keep the baby," I hurried to explain. "And I am not sure I can do it on my own. Would you help me?"

He shrugged, but I could see the disappointment in his eyes. "I can get a sub for the shop tonight and tomorrow. One of my barber college buddies is always begging to work there. Usually I'd want to supervise, but I feel pretty good about him, so yes. I'll stay here."

He gave a long pause. "Why are they doing that anyway?"

"Just one second." I moved my hand and spoke into the phone again. "Brandon came home with me last night."

I heard the sharp intake of breath and continued. "To help with the baby.

"Yeah, sure. I bet he was helpful."

"Don't be a jerk. And keep me posted if you find out anything about the baby's parents, all right?"

"I'll stop by later and check in. Make sure you're doing all right. Try not to be naked when I arrive."

"Uh, yeah. With a baby in the house. That's sure to happen. I'll see you later."

His laughter was cut off when I clicked disconnect."

Turning back to Brandon, I gave him a helpless look. "I guess we're on for the weekend."

He grinned, despite his former sad expression. "Could be worse, I guess."

Whew. He probably wouldn't feel that way after I told him why the authorities thought I was a good risk.

I intended to tell him over breakfast, then after breakfast, then over lunch, but between eating, cleaning up, and figuring out how to care for our little charge—because Brandon had more knowledge than me, but not that much more—the time flew and by four o'clock that afternoon, I had done no more to clear up matters.

I was in the bathroom, wiping spit-up off my T-shirt when I heard the doorbell ring.

"I'll get it," called Brandon in that hushed yell everyone on TV used to avoid waking sleeping babies. "Hey, Ted. Come to make sure we didn't do anything stupid?"

"Something like that. Where's Axel?"

"Here I am." I came out shirtless, having given up on the sour-smelling mess. "Just let me get dressed."

"I thought I warned you about that, Counselor?"

And just like that...the cat was out of the bag.

Chapter Eight

Brandon

I heard the word counselor, but tried like hell not to flinch. Axel shot a look my way but then rushed off to the bedroom and came back minutes later with jeans and a tight gray T-shirt stretched over his pecs.

For the time being, I would ignore the word spoken by the starched police officer and go on about my business of taking care of the little tyke.

"I brought over some things. I stopped at the store and picked out some pajamas, hats, and socks. That's all they need when they're this little." He held out the bag, and Axel took it from his hands.

"Thanks. Now we don't have to wear this anymore."

I put the babe on the couch beside me and took off the raggedy outfit he'd spent too much time in already. "I need to get something to wash him with."

"Here, I'll watch him," Axel said, coming to kneel down next to the couch. I got up and went to the bathroom. After grabbing a washcloth, I ran it under some warm water and found a bar of soap and rubbed it on the cloth. It wasn't the most baby smelling scent in the world, but he would be clean.

When I came out, Axel and Ted were speaking on soft tones, and both turned to me as I entered. Either they were talking about me, or they were talking about something that was none of my business.

"I'm just going to get him cleaned up."

I took a seat next to the babe and cleaned him up the best I could. I wished we had a bathtub with sweet-smelling baby wash, but we didn't. Every baby deserved that.

"There we are. Clean and warm again. Come on up here." I cuddled the babe against my chest. "Do you mind if I walk out in the backyard? I could use some fresh air." I pushed the question to Axel. I did need some fresh air, but more than that, I wanted to give those two a chance to openly talk about whatever they needed to without the threat of me interrupting.

"No, here, let me show you the way."

He walked me through the kitchen and past the laundry room. He opened the door for me and pressed his hand against the small of my back as I went through. It wasn't until the door shut behind me that I allowed myself to breathe again.

"Look at this yard, will you?" I spoke to the babe. "A hot tub and an outdoor kitchen. Impressive."

I found a swing at the corner of the expansive yard and sat down. It had been quite a while since I enjoyed the morning sun. I was usually fast asleep alone in my bed with earplugs to drown out my roommates' chaos.

I looked down at the babe. "I've decided to call you Braxton. It's a little bit Brandon and a little bit Axel, but don't tell him. His ego might explode."

The babe smiled a bit in his sleep. I pretended he understood what I was saying.

"What's this about exploding?" Axel said, and I jumped. I hadn't realized he was approaching. The truth was, I was exhausted. We had to find somewhere for this babe to lie other than in a person's arms.

"Nothing. I was talking nonsense to this babe. I think I have an idea."

He sat next to me on the swing. "What would that be?" He trailed a finger along Braxton's cheek, and I wished it were mine instead.

"It involves a laundry basket, a firm pillow, and a blanket."

I don't know what Axel was thinking about, but redness crept into his cheeks. "What for?"

I chuckled. "A makeshift baby bed. I need some

sleep and a shower. I can't hold this little one twenty-four hours a day."

He swallowed, and I watched his Adam's apple bob. When I let my gaze rise, I saw his eyes on my lips. "I have those things. Let's go inside."

Inside, we set up the laundry basket baby bed in the living room. Axel loaned me some clothes, and I headed off to his shower since he claimed that was the only one that had shampoo, soap, and he'd taken out an extra toothbrush for me.

He turned to leave the bathroom after showing me everything. "My T-shirts are in the top dresser drawer, but help yourself to anything you like."

"Hey, Axel," I called after him.

"Yeah?"

"Maybe after I shower we could…" I didn't get a chance to finish my sentence before he'd returned.

"We could what?" Lust filled the air and hung between us, at least on my end.

"We could talk about why Ted called you counselor."

I didn't wait for his response but instead shut the door to the bathroom and shucked my clothes.

Something was up.

A sinking feeling turned my stomach.

I didn't think Axel was who he said he was at all.

Chapter Nine

Axel

Counselor...

Damn, he'd heard that. All my plans of telling him myself when the time seemed appropriate flew out the window. I looked down at the baby I cuddled in my arms. "Come on, little guy, let's go find that laundry basket and see if you won't take a short nap."

Brandon hollered from the bathroom, "His name is Braxton."

"Okay." I closed the bedroom door behind me and headed for the living room. "You know, Braxton, that's kind of a cute name. Anyway, I wanted to discuss with you the best way to get myself of out the big pickle I'm in. You see, Foster Daddy Brandon just found out I'm not a truck driver and I'm afraid he's not going to like me."

The baby made reassuring little cooing sounds as I explained the whole thing, and while he didn't offer any advice, he was a great listener. Ten minutes later, he was sound asleep in his laundry basket bed, and I was sitting on the couch chewing on my thumbnail, a habit I'd broken when I graduated from law school in order to have neat nails for handshakes with clients and other lawyers.

I heard him approaching but didn't stand or turn my head. I did put my hands in my lap, self-consciously not wanting him to see the ragged nail. Not that he'd care about that, probably he'd be much more concerned with my deceit. And since he'd been clear about his opinion of snooty suits, especially of my ilk, any interest he'd had in me would be gone.

"Mind if I join you?" His voice was so quiet and calm, nothing like his usual cheery tone.

"Please, sit." I waited for him to lower the boom, trying not to take it as too good a sign that he wore a pair of my flannel pj pants and a plain white T-shirt of mine. I was a little taller, and he was a little more muscled, but overall not a bad fit. Also, if he was in pajamas, he wasn't planning to head out and abandon me quite yet.

Of course, that would be for the baby's sake.

He plopped down on the couch, but left a pillow between us. "So, counselor, is that what they are calling long-haul truckers these days?"

I honestly couldn't remember when the lie started. I hadn't made it up. "Uh, no."

"Yeah." He leaned back, but managed not to look relaxed. "I didn't think so."

A long silence ensued during which he kept his gaze focused on our laundry-basket baby, and I tried to use all my lawyerly skills to come up with a convincing opening argument. It was hard with images of him dating a real trucker or maybe some other hard-working blue-collar guy, flashing in my mind. What was wrong with my job? I worked damn hard to make it through law school and achieve my status in a prestigious company.

So what if I hated my current position as lapdog to the CEO of a company who needed a lawyer to handle all the lawsuits related to their bestselling products?

Shaking my head, I prepared to speak but just then Brandon faced me, and the words were gone. Excuses, protests, clever turns of phrase, none of those were needed here. Maybe I might try a little honesty instead. Not a typical tool for my work, especially at the moment, but what the heck. "I never intended to deceive you, but I've heard you say many times how little respect you have for lawyers, and I didn't want you to hate me."

There it was, bald and out there for the world to see.

He blinked. "Are you saying it's my fault you lied to me?"

"I didn't...well I guess I lied by failing to correct your misconception. To be fair, I never actually told anyone I was a truck driver. Someone started the rumor, and when you said you liked blue-collar guys, I just never said different."

"So you lied." His voice rose and the baby squeaked. "Is that true, *counselor*?" he said in a lower tone.

"I guess if we were before a judge and jury, I could be convicted of fibbing."

"Is fibbing a legal term?" The corner of Brandon's lips twitched and I went in for the closing argument.

"I stand, well, sit before you a humbled man, determined never to give you the wrong impressions of me again. The problem remains that you hate lawyers, and I don't know why, but I am an attorney and as much as I want you not to hate me, I'd make a terrible truck driver. You've been out on some of our rides. I have a lead foot."

He narrowed his gaze. "You do always lead the pack. You didn't speed on the way here last night, though."

I shrugged. "Baby on board. But unless you think

Braxton wants to take on long-haul trucking, I probably shouldn't go out and buy a semi."

Brandon sucked in a breath. "You actually could do that, couldn't you? I mean most of the guys I know spend almost all the money they make on truck payments, but you could just go out and buy one cash."

"Maybe, I don't know what they cost, but I have a nice 401k and some savings. Brandon, I might as well get it all out there. I'm a partner in a large, and, yeah, prestigious firm. I make a lot of money. Please don't hate me."

He grinned and looked around. "I can't say that having extra money isn't appealing. I'm saving to buy a little place of my own to get out from under the roommate situation. It's so quiet here."

I had to struggle not to suggest he just move in. I wasn't here all week anyway, and I loved having him in my place. But now was not the time. "Anyway, can you forgive me for being a lawyer?"

"And a liar?"

Now I was trying to smile, for fear he'd think I wasn't taking my perfidy seriously enough. "Can we go with fibber?"

"Sure." He thrust out a hand. "If you promise not to do it again."

I shook his hand, but I wanted to do so much more.

Then the baby woke and cried, and the moment was lost. At least I'd gotten my secret out there. But I still didn't know why he hated lawyers.

Chapter Ten

Brandon

One day I would have to tell him the story, but it wouldn't be now. Brax began to yell like someone had pinched him.

I scooped him up right away and changed his diaper, the culprit of his woes.

After getting dry and having a little cuddle, he was fine again, but fully awake.

I never did get that nap.

I laughed at myself. I guess we were kind of exactly like newborn parents. Awkward, exhausted, and new to all of this.

"What are you laughing at?"

I shrugged, still giving him a little cold shoulder. "I was just thinking this is how new parents are. Tired—cranky—and jumping at every noise the infant makes. This must be what it's like."

Axel's eyes widened and then relaxed.

Some of my hopes for us to be together had faded during our conversation and ever since I heard the word counselor.

We could play house this weekend, but I didn't think the scenario would ever happen in real life. Though, he did say he carried the rumor because I liked blue-collar guys, which I did.

My heart sank as I sat and rocked the babe back and forth as he lay on my knees. My expectations were getting in the way.

"Do you like music?" he asked and then rolled his eyes, I presumed at his silly question.

I snorted. "Are there people who don't?"

He got up and opened a cabinet to reveal a record player. People now called it vinyl, but my dad had one, so, to me, it would always be a record player.

"Is this okay?" He held up a Creedence Clearwater Revival record and waved it back and forth.

"That's actually really good. Lost my virginity to Creedence. One of the songs, not the band." I cracked myself up sometimes. I shrugged. I'd blame it on loss of sleep if he said a damned word.

"So Creedence gets you going, is that what you're trying to tell me?" Axel put the record into the player and moved the needle until I heard a scratching sound.

I spoke to the baby like a coward instead of looking at him. "No, that's not what we were saying, was it? Nope. Just stating a fact. We love Creedence.

Don't we, Braxton?"

Braxton's eyes were drooping. What a life. Sleep, eat, poop, repeat.

I rocked him to the music coming from speakers that probably cost more than my rent for the year while Axel brought in two glasses of ice water and set one next to me.

It took two more songs for the babe to really fall asleep then I laid him in the basket.

I stood and turned to attempt to take a nap on Axel's cushy sofa but when I turned, he was standing so close that our chests touched.

"What?" I asked and almost took a step back, but he grabbed me around the waist.

"May I have this dance?"

No sleep. His clothes. Baby on board, and this alpha wanted to dance.

Consider me thoroughly swooned.

"Um, sure."

He led me to the center of the living room and pressed a button on a remote to change the song to some sultry jazz number. In one tug, we were again chest to chest.

"I'm really sorry about lying or keeping up the lie. I want you to trust me."

I nodded and swallowed. His eyes followed the motion of my throat.

"Why?" I asked breathy as fuck.

"Why do I need you to trust me?"

I nodded.

His eyebrow arched. "Because the lawyer thing was the one thing that's stopped me from bringing you home every time I've seen you for months, and now that it's out of the way..."

He rocked his hips into mine, and it sent a jolt of passion directly to my cock.

I bit down on my bottom lip and chuckled. "You have really bad timing."

He glanced over my shoulder then leaned forward and whispered in my ear, giving me shivers. "I know. I'm sorry. I promise to make it up to you if you'll let me."

I expected him to pull back, but instead he kept his head right there on my shoulder and hugged me tighter as we swayed to the music. I laid my head against his chest. His heart drummed against my ear, fluttering as was my stomach.

This was the moment I'd dreamed about—hoped for—and now it was happening.

"You feel so good in my arms, omega."

The name slipped from his lips and poured over me.

"I know I do."

He laughed and the sound shook us both. "The first time you shaved me, and I felt your hardness on my arm, I wanted to throw you over my shoulder and take you right there in the shop's back room."

He moved his hands to my ass and kept them there. Four, maybe five songs played while we swayed together.

This was all wrong.

We should've been alone and on our first date.

I sighed.

"I know. It's a shame we're not alone. But now that we're past this lawyer thing, you'll let me date you, right?" He pulled back and looked at me from one eye to the other, searching for his answer.

"Yes." Seriously, I needed to work on a sex hotline with that voice that came out around Axel.

Chapter Eleven

Axel

We danced for a long time, or exactly the length of Braxton's nap. I should have kissed him sooner because just as my lips were descending toward his, the impatient wail of a hungry baby cut through the moment.

We jumped apart as if we had been caught doing something wrong. A baby certainly made for an excellent chaperone. Brandon flew to his side, making soothing sounds. "It's okay, Brax. Daddy Axel will make you a bottle right now, won't you Daddy Axel?"

I'd already been on my way to the kitchen to do just that, but those words froze me in my tracks. Daddy Axel? We were just watching the little guy for a short time, for the weekend. How could that have escalated to my being a daddy?

And even while I stood there, facing away from the duo, listening to Brandon talk to Brax while changing his diaper and putting on fresh jammies—narrating each thing he did as he went along—I knew I wanted more than anything in my life to be just that. Daddy

Axel to this little person.

But it was ridiculous to be attached so soon. He had parents, and probably dropping him off at the club had been a huge mistake on the part of an overwhelmed *daddy* of his own. Any minute, the phone would ring, and the police would let us know that they'd straightened out the whole mess. Or a real, certified foster family would be found and he'd be scooped up and taken away to someone else.

I forced my feet to move into the kitchen where I prepared the bottle and made sure it was just the right temperature. My mind was flying, trying out different scenarios. I worked eighty, ninety hours a week Monday through Friday, and I did it out of town. So unless I hired a manny to care for him, I couldn't take him. And Brandon lived with roommates who didn't sound baby friendly.

Really there was only one solution, if they both wanted to keep the baby at least until permanent arrangements were made. I carried the bottle into the living room and traded the bottle for the dirty diaper. Returning to sit on the couch, I prepared to make my argument. "So, how would you like to live here?"

He lifted his face from where he'd been watching the baby eat, his eyes wide. "I beg your pardon?"

62

Oh shit. Not that I wasn't hoping this would lead to something, but I didn't want to rush either one of us. He'd think I was insane to suggest we live together before we'd even kissed. Something I intended to remedy asap. "I mean, if we can arrange to foster the baby, would you mind staying here to do that?"

Was that disappointment in his expression? But he only said, "Brax is worth any sacrifice, even staying here at Palace Axel." Then he grinned, tipping the bottle higher so the baby didn't get any air. "Do you think it could be arranged?"

"I don't know. But maybe an emergency certification could be arranged. I have a clean record, and I assume you don't have any human trafficking convictions or anything?"

"Not me. But you work in the city and I work at night..."

I shrugged. "I can work from here for a week or two, and then after that we can always get a babysitter." And it would give me a chance to spend lots of time with Brandon. Now that he agreed not to hold my job against me...I really needed to know why he felt that way. "What do you say?"

He set the empty bottle on the coffee table and handed me the baby to burp. We were already doing pretty well for amateurs. "If you can get the powers that be to agree, I'm willing to give it a try. At the very least, we're giving him a stable home for a short time. Do you think you can do it?"

I laid Brax on his tummy, a technique I'd seen on the videos, and rubbed his back. "I do think so. I know you don't love what I do but it pays really well, and the authorities tend to respect that." A loud burp rewarded my efforts. "Even if they shouldn't sometimes."

An arched brow was his only response, for which I was grateful.

"Here. If you don't mind taking over with Brax, I'll make some calls and see what I can arrange. You're sure about this, right?" Even I wasn't sure what "this" meant. Because the baby was the most important person in this arrangement, but I couldn't ignore the obvious other possibilities. Could I talk Brandon into moving to the city? They needed barbers there, too...

But I was jumping ahead of myself. With a kiss on the baby's forehead and, after a second's hesitation, a peck on Brandon's parted lips, I headed for my office. First call to Ted...who was delighted and promised to pass along my request to the chief. From his attitude, I guessed they'd hoped to hear from us. They had nothing on the baby's moms and or dads...the camera outside Principal Ink had gotten the person walking up, but they'd worn a hoodie that concealed most of their face, and hadn't gotten into any vehicle within camera range, so unless someone reported a baby missing, they had nothing so far.

I marveled at how the highway officers and town force cooperated here in Roseville. In the city, they would never have worked together so closely on a case like this, at least not if the newspaper stories were accurate. Would they find the parents, and if they did, what next? Since I didn't work in family law and it had been a number of years since law school, I hesitated to guess at the procedures from this point.

But I had lots to do if I was going to work from Roseville for a couple of weeks. As long as my client was out of the country, it should work. And after all the calls...I was going to order in something great for dinner and see if I had another CCR album.

Chapter Twelve

Brandon

He spent more than an hour on the phone in that office. I stayed out because even though he'd asked me to live here, temporarily or whatever we were doing,

For the baby, of course.

That part of the deal was the letdown of it all. He only wanted me here because I had some experience with babies.

But then I thought about when we danced, and I knew that wasn't the truth.

He just didn't know how to say it.

I would have to make sure in no uncertain terms that he knew I was open to more than being his baby helper.

Braxton was an easy baby. My brother Finn had been a holy terror, so I knew the difference. My dad could never get him to stop crying.

Turned out, he was allergic to dairy and so, once that stopped, his crying stopped as well.

Then Dad felt bad for calling him that.

I laid Brax in his bed, which we needed to do

something about, and mulled over this situation. I needed answers. Would there be rent? Could I afford it? I should go to my place and get my things from my apartment and give them notice. Come to think of it, my lease was up the next month, so that would be easy.

Where would I sleep? Where would Braxton sleep?

How would I sleep during the day?

So many questions.

Plus, I should probably get some of my own clothes at some point. I loved walking around in his sweats, enveloped by his scent, but that couldn't last forever.

I heard the door to his office shut while I walked around the house, stretching my legs and trying to relieve some boredom. I didn't watch much TV at home, simply because I didn't feel like fighting my roommates for the remote, so I read tons and tons of books. But my Kindle was at home.

I sighed and waited for him.

"Hey," Axel said, and I yelped even though I'd been listening intently for him.

"Hey, what's the news?"

"I know some people, and they are pulling strings. I've called in all the favors. We should have emergency foster care certification by Monday morning."

I sighed and yet, my nerves came back full force, turning my stomach. That meant I was really here for the near future.

"That's good. At least he won't go into the system."

He nodded and bit his bottom lip while I watched. "Should we talk about some things?"

I whispered yes and the doorbell rang. "Who is that?"

A gleam shone in his face. "Dinner."

He rushed to the front door, pulling his wallet from the counter as he did. He met the delivery person at the door, a young man, I could see from my perch, who spent way too much time making sure his customer was satisfied. Axel laughed at something he said, and a shot of jealousy shot through me.

I waited, deciding to go in to the kitchen and lean on the marble island while I heard him wish the man goodbye.

"I got a little of everything. I hope you like these burgers. They are my favorite." He hadn't even opened the bag, but the scent of grilled meat along with cheese and french fries touched my nose, and hunger awakened my stomach.

"Yeah, I'm not really picky."

He laid out the contents of the bag. There were at least five variations of burgers and two of each, plus curly fries, regular cut fries, and one order of onion rings. "Pick your poison."

I chose the double mushroom and Swiss one, while he chose the barbeque one and stuck some onion rings under the bun before taking a bite. A huge drop of sauce stuck to the side of his mouth, and I grabbed a napkin and wiped it off. When I did, he covered my hand with his and winked at me.

Heat and need pooled in my thighs, and I shuddered.

"These are really good. Thank you."

He took another bite but never dropped his gaze from me.

"I have some questions, maybe things we need to discuss."

"Shoot," he quipped back, popping a fry in his mouth.

"How much rent do I need to pay? I can't afford a lot."

He finished chewing, took a sip from his water bottle, and then reached in the fridge to get me one as well. "None, actually. I own this house outright. I'm...I'm not bragging but I'm very good with my money."

Which was easy when you had plenty of it.

"Okay, well, I have to contribute some way."

He chewed on it and another bite of his burger. Every time he raised it to his mouth, his biceps bulged and so did my dick.

"You are helping take care of the babe. That's enough."

Definitely something we would have to talk about later.

"Where will I sleep? Where will Braxton sleep? We need to get him a crib and set up something more permanent than a laundry basket."

Axel paused. "I have a small room next to my bedroom, a sort of sitting room. That can easily be changed to a nursery. We can order a crib and whatever else he needs online."

He didn't answer the first question, and there was no way in hell I was asking again.

"Okay." At least some things were settled.

We ate the rest of our food in silence. We stole glances and smiles, and every once in a while we would bump elbows or need to brush past each other to get something.

I loved this dance more than the one before.

"Done?" he asked and turned to me.

"I am. I'm actually stuffed."

I leaned over to see Brax still sleeping in his basket. Maybe he was settling in better than me.

"Good. Now, about that question you asked earlier." My stomach flipped, and my insides turned molten. "I'm hoping you'll be in my bed, omega."

Chapter Thirteen

Axel

"I'm hoping you'll be in my bed, omega..." I watched him carefully to see his reaction. I knew I was taking a risk. Moving too fast, perhaps, but I'd have had to be a fool not to recognize the not remotely subtle flirtations at the barbershop over the past months. He surely learned in barber college how to not press his dick into the client under most circumstances.

He reached out and stroked my beard. "I've wondered for a long time if you'd let me hold onto this while you fuck me."

Oh. Hell. "Let's find out." I scooped him up in my arms and carried him into the living room where Brax slumbered in his basket.

"Wait." Brandon patted my arm. "We can't leave him here while we're in your room. Bend over and I'll grab him."

I bent and my omega grasped the basket handles. "I feel a little uncomfortable about, umm, anything with him right there though." Yet I continued on toward my bedroom, now carrying my whole family. Was there anything more alpha than that?

"We can put his bed in the sitting room and leave the door open a little, can't we?"

"Yes." Great idea because if I had to find a babysitter every time we had sex, it was going to even outstrip my budget. Plus, I didn't know a sitter, and couldn't wait. "We'll just have to be quietish."

"We can try." He peered into the basket he held where the baby dreamed on. "But parents have been making more babies for years, and I don't think tiny people like Brax even notice. My folks had us all about a year apart..."

I kicked open my door and headed right past my bed and into the little adjoining room where I clicked on a small reading light. At present it held a love seat, a small table I occasionally used as a desk, and a forty-two-inch flat-screen TV/monitor. I let Brandon slide to stand and as he found a cozy corner to set his basket, I considered my sitting room. Turned out, I wasn't unplugging nearly as much as I thought I was if I had to have two separate places in my relaxing country cottage to do onscreen meetings.

"I think we've got a while; he seems completely out." He rested his hand on my chest. "If you haven't changed your mind?"

"What was it you said about me fucking you?" I grasped his wrist and moved his palm to my pants. "Does this feel like I've changed my mind?"

"No." He shook his head slowly. "I'd say we're of one mind." Brandon turned and walked through the door, shedding his clothes as he went. "But we're still dealing with limited time." He faced me, wearing only his undershorts, while I remained in the doorway between the rooms, watching his speed-striptease.

Despite the need for speed, I took a moment to enjoy the sight. The glow from the lamp cast shadows over what was one heck of hot bod. Toned muscles rather than the bulging kind, but I never liked the bodybuilder type anyway. He looked like the statue of a young Greek I'd seen at a museum in Athens once, and I remembered thinking he was my ideal, as he had likely been the sculptor's. Wondering who he was.

Now I wondered if he was reincarnated in the young barber whose hands flexed at his sides, as my gaze trailed past the tented underwear and down straight, lightly furred legs.

"Alpha?" His voice shook only a little. "If you aren't going to get over here and do me, you're going to have to watch me do myself."

And wasn't that also a good idea. Just not now. "I'll take a rain check because I really do want to see that." I swallowed past my dry throat as I also stripped down to next to nothing. Then, holding his gaze, I grasped the waistband and pulled off my shorts. He reached for his, as well, but I shook my head. "No. Let me." Three steps brought me to stand in front of him, and, as I worked his underwear down his legs, his dick bobbed free, long and straight and already glistening with precum. "Oh, very nice." Unable to resist, I dropped to my knees and, wrapping my fist around his length, bent to lap the fluid from the tip. Salty and heady with musk.

"Do we have time to...ohhhh." Brandon braced his palms on my shoulders as I took him into my mouth, a bit at a time, retreating then going deeper...savoring the pleasure of having him so close, of the scent and sight of him, of learning with my lips and tongue his shape and texture.

When I had him in my throat, I sucked hard, loving his gasps and moans. His balls swung, and I cradled them in my palm, stroking them with my thumb, feeling for the moment when it was almost but not quite too late.

His grip on my shoulders tightened, fingers

digging in, and I let him slip from my lips, licking his flavor from them.

A little push and he sat on the edge of my king-sized bed, legs sprawled wide, just as I wanted them. "Ready for me to fuck you?"

He grabbed my beard.

A groan-chuckle spilled from me. How could he make me laugh while at the same time making me so hard? Moving between his thighs, I bent them back toward his chest then stroked two fingers through his hot, slick readiness. "I guess you are ready." Another time I'd suck him dry, but when he gave a tug on my beard, I positioned my cock and thrust deep into his hot, tight ass. No more laughter, just groans from both of us as I plunged in and retreated, over and over, fighting the urge to spill instantly. Still, it wouldn't be long.

His dick bobbed between us, an invitation I grasped when I closed my fist around it and stroked, hard, tight, up, down, release, matching the rhythm of my cock inside him. All too soon my balls tightened, and my cum poured into his body. He jerked and then followed, his creamy white semen flowing over my hand, coating his belly, intensifying the scent of both our arousal.

And I knotted.

I hadn't intended to, in fact, never had before...but I swelled to fill him, stretching him wider, the level of pleasure rising so high, I almost blacked out. Shuddering, I braced my hand on the bed so I wouldn't crush him then rolled to the side, taking him with me, our bodies tangled together, and he let go of my beard, flung his arms around my neck, and kissed me.

Warm, sweet, heavenly kisses that went on until my knot receded and my cock slid free.

Two seconds later, a wail pierced the air, and our moans were of a different kind.

"I think it's your turn, alpha," Brandon muttered, his eyes fluttering closed.

Such a couple thing to say.

I stopped in the adjoining bathroom for a moment to clean up then grabbed a pair of clean shorts from the dresser before heading into the baby's room to take him and his basket downstairs for a change and a bottle.

Next time, in a few hours...it would be my omega's turn.

Chapter Fourteen

Brandon

I lay there listening to Axel as he picked up the babe and cooed to him that everything would be okay. Spreading my arms above my head, reveling in pure bliss, I felt all filled up. Filled with satisfaction, relief that Axel wanted me, his seed, and...love.

I'd keep that last one to myself.

"I'm going to make him a bottle," Axel said. I still had my eyes closed. I decided to take a shower while he was busy and was toweling off when he came into the room minutes later, Brax cradled in his arms with a bottle in his mouth.

He grinned at me, and I felt the warmth of a blush heat me from head to toe. "You know, if this was normal dating stuff, I would've joined you for that shower, happily."

I chuckled and moved to kiss Brax on the forehead and then pecked Axel on the lips. "Yeah, well, we'd better get used to the cock blocking. It's bound to be a regular thing."

He leaned forward and kissed me again. "But not

too much. I already know we need a babysitter."

I put on the pants I wore before, not bothering with a shirt. "I also need to go get my things."

He nodded. "I know. Ted said he put a car seat by the front door so we can go do that tomorrow—or tonight if you need to."

I hadn't realized Ted had done that, otherwise, I would've had Axel drive me over there right away. It wasn't that I didn't like being in his clothes, I did. But I wanted my own stuff.

"No, tomorrow morning is fine. I need to give my roommates notice anyway. They need time to find a replacement."

"Did you want to watch a movie up here while this one finishes up his bottle?"

I nodded, but when I looked at the bed, a swarm of lust filled my thoughts. I cleared my throat as his gaze followed mine. "Maybe we should go downstairs to the couch so we can behave."

He scrunched up his nose. "You don't think a change of location will make me behave, do you? But we can try." He winked at me, and I melted. I walked downstairs first, and he slapped my ass while I passed. "See? I'm just out of control."

I chuckled. "You're just a bunch of secrets."

"How is that?"

We sat next to each other on the couch, and I took Brax from him to burp him halfway through the bottle. "Well, at the shop people think you're a truck driver, tough, hot, and rugged, but you're really a lawyer in a suit. And I would guess that people at your office think you're this stuck-up attorney, but really you're an alpha who likes to have his beard tugged while he talks dirty."

"Well, as long as you know the truth, I don't give three shits what anyone else thinks about me. So, murder, documentary, or comedy?"

"Um, whatever. I don't really care. I guess one day we'll be watching educational shows."

That was a big assumption on my part—that we would be together when Brax was old enough to enjoy shows like that.

"Probably so. I'm not watching *Sesame Street*, for the record. They took away Big Bird, and I just can't."

I laughed loud and hard, startling Braxton. "I didn't realize you and the yellow bird were so close."

He chuckled. "Well, now you know. Oh, there's a new show about witches on."

I didn't think a show about witches was really going to rock us to sleep, but I didn't argue. By the time the show was over, Brax was asleep on my chest, and Axel rubbed my feet on his lap.

I was exhausted but not sleepy, not a good place to be.

"You need some sleep, Brandon."

"Probably." I glanced at the time. This was usually when I would be taking my lunch hour on my regular schedule. "But I'm not sleepy."

"Okay, one more episode. Let me go get his basket. I'm needing to cuddle you some more."

I looked at him down my nose. "I thought we were behaving."

He shrugged and then bounced up the stairs. "I am—probably."

"I'm in trouble, Braxton. Big, big trouble and even our lawyer wouldn't be able to get me out of it. Daddy Axel has me wrapped around his finger," I murmured to the babe before Axel came back down.

"Come here, little man." He took Brax from me and, after some sweet kisses on his head, put him down in the basket. "Now, you come here, big man."

He sat and patted his lap. "On your lap?"

"Yep. Best place to watch a movie."

He moved to sit with his back to the side of the couch and I sat on top, our legs tangled together. Axel stroked my hair, and I laid my head on his chest.

I didn't hear one word of the next episode because after a few minutes of listening to his breaths, sleep took over whether I wanted it to or not.

Chapter Fifteen

Axel

We spent Sunday moving Brandon's stuff into my house, not that it took the whole day. My barber omega had very few personal belongings, in part because the corner of the living room he called his own was about the size of a twin bed. Although I doubted he made a fortune at the shop, I figured he took in more in tips than his share of the rent in this slum-style apartment.

He'd tried to make me wait outside, but I didn't, of course, wanting to help carry things. And what I saw made me even gladder he was coming to live with me. His little corner of the apartment was an island of clean in a sea of filth. Fast-food wrappers, beer bottles, overflowing ashtrays... We'd left the baby with Ranger, the owner of Principal Ink, while we moved.

When we were back in his car and headed for my place, I asked the question. "Why do you live like this?" He didn't seem like someone who'd lived rough before. He spoke well, like someone who'd had a good education, and had better table manners than mine. I'd wager I could give him an array of twenty pieces of silverware at the table and he would never ask which fork. Why would he choose to dwell in such circumstances?

"It's not so bad. I work a lot, and hang out at the club, so I'm almost never here anyway." He turned to look out the passenger window, chewing on his thumbnail.

"Uh-huh." I drove away from that place with the last of his things in the trunk, only the second load even though he'd had some things in the shared storage area. I knew there was more to the story but didn't feel I could push any harder just now. "Anyway, have you ever been to the candy store on Main Street? I think it's called Sugar or something?"

Apparently I'd said the right thing to change the subject to a more positive topic. He jerked around in the seat, jaw dropping. "You haven't been to Sugar yet?" Apparently shocking news. "People come from hours away to buy Liam's candy and treats. We have to remedy that right now." We were just pulling up in front of Principal Ink, and I parked, carefully, between a Harley Softail and a kind of impressive 1970s era Honda 1000. "Braxton probably hasn't been yet, either. We can't have a Roseville kid with that big gap in his cultural education."

The child in question was being carried out of Principal Ink by Ranger, surrounded by a bunch of bikers in leather and denim. One bearded guy I'd seen there a few times was letting our little boy hold his finger while he made funny faces and Brax laughed. Brandon hopped out and took the baby then buckled him in his seat before taking his place again. "Jerry is sure crazy about our little guy."

"Jerry?" I hadn't really talked with the guy before but something tickled my memory. "Wasn't he part of some fairly radical gang? Convicted of something or other?"

"Oh yeah. But he did his time. He had a substance abuse problem, primarily, and stole to feed it."

"Maybe it's not a good idea to have Brax babysat there." I'd never considered the dangers the club—but then I'd never had a baby to care for before. "I mean...they are not exactly Sunday school teachers or anything but—"

"Jerry is." Brandon fastened his seat belt. "Head for Main Street."

"Wait." I rested my hand on the gear shift. "He is what?"

"A Sunday school teacher. He is also a community leader, head of neighborhood watch for his building,

87

and leads a charity auction every year to raise funds for the community center, My Brother, My Sister. He also teaches MMA class there on Saturday. For free."

"Really?"

"Yep, turn left here." I made the turn, and he went on. "He's kind of a standout, but Ranger doesn't want any trouble at PA, and neither do any of the others, so if someone is involved, currently at least, in anything unsavory, he shows them the door. They call him the Principal for a reason."

"I thought it was because he used to be one."

"Here's Sugar. Park around back." Brandon flashed a grin over the seat at Brax. "You're too little to eat the candy, yet, buddy, but there's a lot to see there."

I did enter the parking lot and select a space, but before I turned off the engine, I asked, "But what about getting you settled at home? We can always come back and buy some candy." After all, it was just a store.

"Oh no." He was already out of the car and opening the back door to bring out Brax. "If you're going to be part of Roseville, you have to visit Sugar. It's unique."

I gave up and followed him around to the front door of the business. "Do they have fudge?" I asked. It

Lorelei M. Hart

was my greatest weakness.

He chuckled. "Usually around a dozen flavors on any given day."

I reached for the door handle but he laid his free hand over mine. "You can't just walk into Sugar. It's an experience." Linking our fingers, he tugged me over to stand in front of the big plate glass window. I was sure he had a point, but since my heart was thudding in my ears at his touch, it was a little hard to focus.

"Bears!" Dropping my hand—to my sadness—he hefted Brax higher and turned the baby to face the window. "Gummies! They make the most fabulous giant gummies, all naturally flavored and colored so as soon as he's a little bigger, Brax can try them. Usually they have one or two in their display, but this time it's all about the bears!"

An entire carnival occupied the large display window, featuring a Ferris wheel filled with gummies in all colors, mostly bears, as Brandon said, but I spotted a few other animals like a horse and a cat. The ride was slowly turning, and the roller coaster in front of it was also in action, gummies riding up and down and around. Balloons...gummies, too...and banners, and a funhouse backdrop completed the scene.

"That's amazing." I turned at the baby's happy

89

crow. "You like it, Brax? Do you like the bears?"

"And what's not to like?" A youngish man surrounded by a flock of kids approached down the sidewalk. "Hi, Brandon. This must be the biker baby I've heard so much about."

"Edison." Brandon hugged him while I fought jealousy. "This is Brax. And also, this is Axel, who is taking care of him with me."

We shook hands and spoke of the weather for a moment, but the kids began to shift and one said, "We gonna stand here all day?"

Edison flashed a frown at the boy, but then laughed. "I need to take this crew inside. They won the spelling bee this week and earned a reward. They chose a trip to my alpha's place of business for a treat." With a wink, he ushered them inside.

"I love this town." The words just blurted out on their own, and I clapped a hand over my mouth.

Brandon's smile covered his whole face, his eyes twinkling in a whole new way. "I'm very glad you feel that way, alpha. Now, let's go inside and get a treat ourselves. We've worked hard and earned one."

"After you, omega." And not only because I loved the view of him from the rear. I was an alpha, and a gentleman.

Chapter Sixteen

Brandon

The last two weeks had come and gone like a whirlwind, which was expected when taking care of a baby.

Axel and I had been approved for foster care and given guardianship of Braxton.

But I knew this day was coming, the day when Axel would put on his monkey suit and go into the city and work.

It conjured up all kinds of thoughts—thoughts I didn't want to have but couldn't help because I knew how these things worked, or how they worked with my dad.

He would say he would be in the city working for a week—then a week turned into a month.

My other dad found out he was cheating with his assistant and another lawyer in the firm.

He said he was sorry and groveled his way back into our home, but that time away wreaked havoc on my stay-at-home dad's psyche.

Our family was never the same, and I blamed it all on the fact that my dad was a greedy lawyer.

On the surface, I knew Axel wasn't the same, but we hadn't made any promises beyond taking care of Brax. Yes, he called me omega and I called him alpha, but what were we other than babysitters who slept together at night? I didn't know.

"You're letting your breakfast and your coffee get cold, Brandon." He spoke to me over the kitchen island. He leaned over, braced on his elbows, shirt still unbuttoned and tie wound around his neck but not yet in a knot.

Doom drilled into my chest. Under no circumstances did I want him to go.

Plus, I was antsy. My sub had filled in for me for the last few weeks and would have to for the time being, but I missed my job. I missed getting up and dressing myself in something other than jeans. Really I longed for some time away from this house. Not that it wasn't huge or amazingly comfortable, but a guy needed to get out once in a while.

"It's fine. It doesn't do a lot anymore anyway. I've become immune. What time are you leaving?"

"In about five minutes, in fact. Need anything before I leave?"

I shook my head but mentally answered, "For you to stay."

"Help me with my tie?" he asked, and I couldn't resist him. I hopped up on the counter and spread my legs for him to stand between them. "I'll only be gone for a week, Brandon."

"I know." I made some magic out of his tie knot. I remembered doing that for my dad once upon a time. "We'll be here."

"What's this?" He reached up and wiped my cheek and showed me evidence of a tear. I hadn't realized I was crying.

I shrugged and finished up the knot after buttoning him up all the way to his Adam's apple.

"I'll be home tonight. I hate to leave you like this."

I waved him off and started to unload the dishwasher to hide my expression. "Have a good day. Be safe."

I'd taken a few bottles from the top rack when his arms snaked around my middle and pulled me toward his chest. "I'm not even gone yet and you've turned cold. Don't I get a goodbye kiss?"

I sighed and tried to pull myself together. If he knew how I was unraveling on the inside, he wouldn't move an inch. "I'm not cold—it's just that I'll miss you."

"Look at me, omega." *Omega, not omega mine.*

I turned, still in his embrace, and gazed up at those beautiful blue eyes. "What?"

He nipped at my bottom lip. "I'm going to miss you terribly, you and Braxton. Don't you know that?"

I certainly did not. Okay, maybe I did—a little. Instead of saying those things, I shrugged.

"Well, I will." He pulled back. "I'm waiting for my kiss."

I grabbed each side of his collar and tugged him down. He chuckled as our mouths met but then turned serious as my tongue teased his mouth open. I rocked my hips into his, hoping my proof of passion would lure him to stay.

"I expect to get kissed like that again when I come home tonight," he said and slapped me on the ass.

"If you come home," I chortled quietly.

"What?"

"Nothing. Be safe."

He nodded, grabbed his briefcase, and I waited until the front door closed before crumpling to the floor in a sobbing mess. I buried my face into my bent knees and wrapped my arms around my legs. That lasted a whole two minutes until my Braxton's cries came through the speaker of the baby monitor Axel had bought last week.

No time for this man to cry.

"I'm coming, tiny one." I gathered myself and stood, swiping at my tears with a rough paper towel, and slammed the dishwasher shut.

When I got to the nursery, Braxton was dirty, wet, red-faced, and hungry. Looked like he was having as great a Monday as I was.

"Come on, you. Let's get into the bath to clean you up then a bottle."

The warm water soothed him back to calm and cleaned him up as well. I sat down with him on the rocking chair Axel had also purchased and fed him. "Daddy Axel is gone to work, buddy. It's just you and me today. Maybe we can go for a walk in your new stroller. What do you think?"

I looked at the time.

He had only been gone an hour, and already I was in dire need of his voice, his arms, his lips, all of him.

Chapter Seventeen

Axel

I did make it home that night in time for dinner to warm hugs and kisses from Brandon and cuddles with sweet-smelling Brax. Actually, they both smelled pretty good. I realized as I opened the door that my home had gone from smelling musty, to smelling like a place where people lived. Cooking food, laundry detergent, baby products...Brandon's cologne, and his own scent. The moment I stepped inside, I was home.

Partway through our two weeks of peace, I'd had a service deliver my car, so I hadn't ridden the bike in and out of the city. That felt odd. And I hadn't stopped by my apartment. Why would I? There were no pets or plants there, and the weekly cleaning service would get rid of any spoiled food in the refrigerator, not that there was much. Nearly all my meals were meetings of one kind or another, the rest merely takeout. A few low-cal frozen dinners for emergencies. No, that house did not smell of food or people. Usually it smelled of cleaning products with a faint echo of my cologne. Not all that pleasant a combo really.

But after my first day in the city, I ate dinner with Brax on my lap, enjoying Brandon's pasta with olives and sun-dried tomatoes from a 1980s recipe site he loved online. Since he followed that up with tiramisu, we ended up on the couch, slumped in front of the vampire show on Netflix we'd been binging on, and, after we put Brax down for the night, we made love in the flickering glow of the screen.

Then got up and did it again. It went pretty well for that first week. I rejected dinner meetings, making them either lunch or breakfast, and managed to get home in time for at least a late supper with my omega and our charge.

The weekend flew by and then began week two. At six o'clock on Monday, I sat at my desk facing the senior partner who requested I join him and the other partners for cocktails at the bar atop our building. I protested, but he insisted, and two vodka martinis later, I'd been informed that my "short" days were going to cost me. As a partner, I had some protection, but as the newest partner, it was limited. And my client had apparently complained that I refused to meet him at ten o'clock that night to discuss something we'd gone over a hundred times already.

Jealousy played a part in the vitriol, I knew,

because any of them would have liked to take over my client. I had him only because I'd gone to school with his son for a while and he remembered me.

Not that he liked me, or I liked him, but he liked manipulating me.

And that is how I found myself in a sushi bar at ten that night, going over the elements of a particular contract between his firm and a competitor, where they were going to swallow the smaller company and pick their teeth with its bones. Not only had we gone over it a hundred times, it was already signed and being implemented.

Manipulation.

Finally, at midnight, I pushed back from the table. "Well, it's been fun, Don," I lied. "But I have to get going. Got the omega and the little guy waiting for me." I hoped he'd figure I was tied down now and show some respect for that. Not that he did with his own family. Don was known to spend as many nights in the arms of his mistresses and side omegas as his husband.

"That's right. I hear you are taking care of some foundling." How had he heard that? Of course, one of the other partners probably couldn't wait to gossip about me. "And you hired an omega? A manny? Very generous of you."

I paused, hand extended to shake. "Ah, not exactly, but more or less. I hope you have a nice rest of the night, and I'll speak with you about that new acquisition tomorrow sometime." Sometime because he'd call or show up at the office—or summon me to his—at his pleasure. I was halfway to the door when I heard his voice and stopped. He was on the phone. And what he said chilled me to the bone.

"That's right. See if you can get that baby for me, Fred. If you can smooth the path, I might see about changing my representation in other areas. My omega is always whining about me working too hard and staying out too late. We haven't been able to pregnant, but a baby would keep the old ball and chain busy and off my back."

He went on, but I didn't wait to hear the rest. A baby to keep his omega off his back. I had no doubt this child he spoke about as if he were no more than a cheap toy was our Brax.

I stumbled to the car, my mind spinning in a hundred directions. First, the baby wasn't available for adoption yet, but there was no reason Don and his omega couldn't be certified, their money would speed up the process and greasing enough palms might also help speed up the adoption possibilities.

Driving out of the city, I put extra pressure on the gas pedal, wanting only to get home to my omega and our child. Sure, only a foster child, for now, but I'd go to any lengths to prevent that snake from using Brax to keep his omega "off his back."

Halfway back to Roseville, red-and-blue lights flashed in my rearview mirror, and I pulled over to the side. Shit, way to make myself the best choice to take care of Brax. The courts were sure to be impressed by my speeding.

And this time it wasn't even Ted.

Chapter Eighteen

Brandon

Axel came in like a hurricane blowing through. Usually a neat person, he dropped his briefcase right at the door, followed by his shoes and his jacket. He even cussed at his tie when he wrestled with it.

"Oh, dear. Daddy Axel has had a bad day. Let's get him a glass of wine," I whispered, not so softly to Braxton who had begun to smile and coo at both of us.

"No wine. I've had enough tonight. Thank you though. Can we just sit together on the couch? I need my boys."

I swallowed against the emotion in my throat and he led us, with his hand on the small of my back, to the couch where we sat close, and he reached over to take Brax from my sore arms. The boy liked to be held, and it was all our fault.

"Hey, my boy. We love you so much." He cuddled Brax next to his chest and rubbed his back while kissing the top of his head.

I had only known this alpha, really known him, for a few weeks, but something was off beyond a late night at work.

"Axel, what's wrong?"

"I got stopped for speeding on the way home. Some dickhead named Officer Kingston. It won't stick, of course. I'll have my buddies take care of it, but still."

Seemed like a petty thing to get so riled up over, but I figured maybe it was the straw that broke the camel's back. For the rest of the night he was a stale, cold mess. When it was time for bed, he got in and hugged me tightly to him but it felt like he was a mile away.

He left the next morning without a word and without waking me, so by the time he got home I had stewed all day.

"What do you want for dinner?" I asked him.

He shrugged and put his arm around my shoulders. "I don't care. Let's order in so you don't have to cook."

I fished my phone from my pocket and ordered through the delivery service. Nothing sounded good to me lately, especially the last two days, so I ordered Axel's favorite—bowls of pho.

"Oh, soup sounds great. Thank you," he said, looking over my shoulder at the order.

"You're welcome. I might not eat, though, I've

been feeling a little weird lately about food."

He made a grunting sound but went back to fawning over the babe. I loved to see him like this, so engrossed in Brax. He was ours, blood or no blood.

"Let's not leave him with anyone else to babysit. It might not sit well with social services."

I felt my eyebrows scrunch. "I only left him that one time."

He shrugged. "That's fine. Just from now on I'd like to keep him ourselves. And I'm going to install a swing in the backyard so you don't have to leave to swing him anymore."

Anxiety swirled in my chest. Something was definitely up.

"Axel, what are you talking about? The park is the only place I go besides the grocery store. I have to get out of here once in a while."

He shrugged. "I know, but it would be safer, don't you think? We have to keep a strict eye on our boy."

He sounded like a robot, spitting out some made-up shit.

My emotions had been out of control lately, but this I couldn't take.

"Are you saying that I don't? If there's something you need to say about the way I take care of Braxton, just spit it out."

"I'm gonna go change out of this suit and then we can talk over dinner." He handed Brax over to me, and I almost seethed.

Are you sure he's safe to leave with me?

By the time the doorbell rang and Axel was still showering and changing, I was livid. He was the one who asked me to move in and help him take care of the babe. If he thought I was so inept, he should've just hired a manny.

I took the bag from the delivery person in one hand while I balanced Brax in the other.

Axel emerged from the bedroom and took the bag from me, but his eyes didn't meet mine.

I couldn't help but be taken back to my parents.

Coming in late—saying awful things—not looking me in the fucking eye.

I put Brax to bed and went back into the kitchen to eat with Axel. He wore no shirt and some basketball shorts that showed me his V, which I was only mildly interested in after his behavior.

Okay, a little more than mildly.

"What's up with you? Just say it."

He hung his head. "Let's eat first."

I whisper shouted, not wanting to wake the babe.

"Bullshit. I can't eat with this hanging over my head. Talk to me. Now."

Despite my argument, he opened the bowls of pho. Usually we both dug in with gusto, but the moment the scent of broth and something seaweed-like hit my nose, I gagged.

Trying to control it, I watched as he swirled the noodles around, and I couldn't help it—it looked like vomit.

And so, I rushed to the bathroom and barely made it before tossing my cookies right into the toilet.

Chapter Nineteen

Axel

Brandon tore out of the room and the bathroom door slammed behind him. By the time I set my spoon down and followed, the sounds from inside the guest bath indicated a seriously upset tummy. I waited for him to take a breath and tapped gently. "Omega, can I come in?"

He cleared his throat. "I'm okay."

Not an answer but I turned the knob anyway, relieved he hadn't locked it. "You don't sound okay to me." Nor did he look it with his arms braced on the seat, head hanging over the bowl. "Is it something you ate?" Couldn't be the pho, since he hadn't had a single bite.

He moved to stand, and I stepped closer and wrapped an arm around him assisting him to his feet. I didn't like his color, either, kind of a greeny beige. He let me help him out of the bathroom and into the bedroom, which I figured was farther from food smells.

"I guess it's the sandwich from lunch. I had half a

tuna...and I don't think I'll ever want that again. Not now that I've seen it return." He sat on the edge of the bed and covered his mouth, paler again.

"If you're okay, I'm going to get you some water...or would you rather have ginger ale?" He slumped back against the pillows, and I lifted his legs onto the mattress.

"Water, I guess. That was humiliating. I guess now you know how attractive I am when I'm sick."

I reassured him that he was hot to me no matter what shade of green, but as I filled the glass at the refrigerator spout, something else occurred to me. Maybe it was the sandwich, or maybe he had some kind of a virus. A virus that might be much worse for a baby. Before heading back to the bedroom, I sent a text to my assistant letting him know I'd be working from home due to illness for the rest of the week. Everyone would assume I was the sick one and I preferred it that way. Most of the firm would let their significant other languish at home sick, vulnerable baby or not...that was not me.

It might have been just a few weeks ago, though.

"Here you go." I walked into the bedroom, hearing my phone ring from the kitchen. But as I stood over my omega, who was a little less green and sound asleep, one arm curled around the pillow, a cry came over the baby monitor, and I set the glass on the nightstand within Brandon's reach and headed back out into the hallway. But instead of turning left, to attend to whichever member of my firm was going to demand I go to work even at death's door, I turned right toward Brax's nursery. Priorities.

Mine had shifted.

By morning, Brandon looked pretty good although he didn't want any breakfast, but I tucked him back into bed and brought him tea and toast anyway, just like my folks brought me when I was a sick little kid. "You have to keep up your strength," I insisted before going to wash my hands thoroughly, as I had every time I'd gone back and forth between the two of them all night. Between checking on Brandon and feeding and changing Brax, I probably had gotten an hour's sleep.

Fortunately, Brax took his bottle, burped, and fell asleep, and I quickly changed into a shirt and tie and headed into my office downstairs for an onscreen meeting. It gave me pleasure that my lower half, hidden by the desk, was clad in sweats and I wore no shoes. The client was very upset to learn I was out of town and not available to meet him for lunch, but since we had nothing to meet about, and it was just more evidence of his desire to take full advantage of the retainer he paid the firm for my time, he could bite me.

I of course didn't say that.

I told him I was contagious with a raging intestinal virus that I could not in good conscience bring either to the office or to him. That not only made him agree he didn't want to see me in person for the next several days, but also gave me a terrific and unquestioned reason to click off after about ten minutes.

With that resolved, I continued my rounds. Check on Brandon, keep him hydrated with endless glasses of water, ginger ale, and lemonade, and feed and change and rock Brax. By five o'clock, when my omega emerged from the bedroom looking much more like himself, I was slumped on the sofa, staring into space.

"Alpha, you okay? You didn't catch my bug, did you?" he asked, sitting in the armchair across from me. I didn't like him so far off, but contagion was a real thing.

I yawned. "I don't think so, but I don't know how you manage to take care of things all day. You must be exhausted."

He grinned. "I take care of the baby and do a little light housekeeping. You have taken care of the baby, of me, of the house, and had at least half a dozen meetings if I heard right. And that was after being up almost all night with us. I think you need a nap."

"You need to go back to bed. And rest. I'll be fine." But the next yawn made my jaw crack.

Brandon gave me a soft smile. "You're not fine at all. And if you get too tired, you'll be sick for sure."

"So you think you had a twenty-four-hour bug?" Not that I was going to the office even if he had.

"Yeah. Now"—he stood and held out a hand to me—"you go sleep and I'll—oh shit. What's that smell?" He yanked the hand back and clapped it over his mouth. Racing off toward the bathroom he yelled, "Maybe forty-eight hours."

I sniffed the air as I followed him. The pho. I'd had it reheating in the microwave. Smelled wonderful to me.

Chapter Twenty

Brandon

I lay in bed after the fifth bout of throwing up and had nothing left inside me to vomit, when it dawned on me like a lead hammer to the forehead.

"Axel, I think we need to consider something other than the flu, alpha."

I added alpha because of the predicament I was now sure we were in.

"Do we need to go to the doctor? What should we consider?" He sat on the edge of the bed and the movement almost made me puke again. I needed stillness and darkness and cold.

"You…" I almost said love or some other cuddly name, but didn't think we were quite there yet. "You need to get to the drugstore and pick up a test."

The color drained from his face. "What kind of test?"

I giggled and then immediately stopped. Everything hurt. "A pregnancy test, you goof."

Axel, big of a man as he was, reached out and held onto the bedpost like he was about to go down next.

"Do you think that's what is happening?"

"Past tense. I think the getting pregnant part already happened."

Gods, I would absolutely shrink if he wasn't happy with the thought. I couldn't bear to look at him to see his reaction. It would potentially break my heart.

"I can run to the store right now. Will you be okay? Should I call Ranger or someone over to watch you?"

"I'll be better once I know what this is. In fact, I will know exactly what to do about it if I am pregnant. Can you also get some Pedialyte?" He looked perplexed. "Just ask the pharmacist for rehydration fluids. His name is Cane."

He nodded and wasted no time running down the stairs and slamming the front door behind him.

I got out of bed and walked slowly, holding onto furniture and walls for strength while I made my way to Brax's room. He was still asleep, but merely being in his presence made me feel better somehow. I lay on the cool floor next to his basket and, before I knew it, fell asleep.

I woke up sometime later to Axel sitting cross-legged in front of me with Brax in his arms taking a bottle. He had come so far from not wanting to hold him to Daddy Axel.

"I got what you asked for. Cane was helpful. How do you know him?"

If I wasn't mistaken, there was a bit of jealousy in his tone. I shifted to sit up slowly, afraid another push of nausea would overtake me. "He was my best friend in high school. We grew apart, but I see him now and again."

That seemed to quell whatever he was feeling. His shoulders slumped and the tightness in his jaw relaxed.

"I'm going to go take that test now. Put both our minds at ease."

His brow furrowed. "What do you mean?"

I shrugged. Maybe I was just being over emotional. "I don't know. You didn't seem very happy about the prospect earlier."

He took my hand in his, balancing Brax. "Omega, it would be an honor for you to carry my babe. Don't ever think I was anything but happy. I'm just very worried about you. I have been for days. It's killing me to see you so sick, even if that sickness is from being pregnant. Let's get clear on that."

I nodded, but didn't quite believe him. What the hell was I going to do? He wasn't here most of the time. The only reason he'd been here lately was because I'd been sick. Now I was supposed to be pregnant and take care of an infant? What would happen to my job? Did he expect me to just end my career and be a homemaker because he made more money?

I sighed and went to the bathroom where not less than ten different pregnancy tests lay on the counter along with every flavor of Pedialyte and Gatorade.

I did the peeing on the stick and with my phone, put a timer for two minutes. I paced up and down the bedroom until the damned timer went off and yelped.

Axel came in and with Braxton in arms, looked at me. "Brandon, should I go look? Let's go look together."

We went into the bathroom, and I turned it over to see two very dark-pink lines.

I sat on the closed lid of the toilet and put my face in my hands.

I was so screwed.

I shouldn't feel this way. I wanted this baby and Brax, but the situation made me feel like I was walking uphill in the snow during a hurricane.

We had to figure some things out.

"Aren't you happy, omega mine?"

I jerked my head up. It was the first time I had ever heard him call me mine, and it totally did me in. Tears flowed from my eyes like a river, which was surprising, considering I was sure I didn't have a drop of liquid left in my system.

"I'm happy and scared," I said between sobs. "We need to work some things out, Axel. I won't live this way anymore—not with another baby on the way."

He touched my hair but then pulled back. "Let me put Brax down and yes, I agree. Those two minutes made me crazy and I know something has to change. Get some of that Gatorade, too. Oh, and, Brandon? I love you."

Chapter Twenty-One

Axel

Loved him?

Hell, yeah, I loved him. I loved him so much I could hardly contain myself. I loved him. I loved that little spark of life inside him. And I loved Brax. I loved him a lot. As that week slid into the weekend, I basked in the glow of our family. No, we hadn't committed to becoming a family, at least not in so many words.

But what else could we be? A ball of tension inside me that never seemed to ease, suddenly had. Sure, I disappeared into my office, upstairs or down to take meetings, but in between, I was cuddling and feeding Brax—thinking how our little person would have the advantage of daddy's milk, but we were buying the best quality formula available, so the pediatrician we visited on Thursday afternoon had complimented us on how good the little one looked. He said Brax was about four months old, and just a little small for his size, but since none of us knew his history, we had no way of knowing what he'd been through to get to this point. The doctor saw no reason he wouldn't catch up size-wise and as far as other milestones, he was grasping toys held out to him, tracking well, and making attempts to roll over. Our little guy was smart as a whip.

Despite my wish to push it back, Monday rolled around, and I was dressed up and on my way out the door after a kiss to each of my family members, including the baby still inside my omega's flat belly. I felt so much better than I had in the longest time, singing along to an oldies station on the commute to the city. We still hadn't figured out how to accommodate Brandon's job but I felt equal to almost any task.

That ended within five minutes of my arrival at work. The receptionist held up a hand as I moved past him. "Your favorite client is waiting in your office, sir."

I paused, irritated. "You mean my only client. Why is he in there instead of the waiting area?"

"The boss saw him arrive and escorted him in. Your PA couldn't stop him."

"No, I suppose not. Well, I appreciate the heads-up." Cary, our receptionist was going to law school at night, but he'd told me confidentially that he wasn't planning to work for a big firm like this. He didn't have the stomach for it. I was beginning to think I didn't either.

Outside my office door, I gave my PA a smile to let him know I wasn't holding this against him then straightened my shoulders and plunged inside. I tried not to let it bother me that I'd had the urge to knock.

"Well, well," I said, striding in with as much confidence as I usually had. "What a pleasant surprise. Did Julian offer you coffee, Lee?"

The man in question lounged on my sofa with his leg crossed over his knee, looking like he owned the place. Or thought he did. "Yes, he offered but you know me. I don't touch the stuff."

"Oh, that's right." He was constantly on some new kick. Last week he'd been drinking something he called bulletproof coffee by the gallon. "Well, anything else? Tea? Sparkling water? Fresh squeezed juice?"

He held up a travel cup. "Got my algae smoothie right here. Tasty stuff. You ever have it?"

"Uh...no but sure sounds good for you." I sat behind my desk, deliberately leaving space between us. "So, did I forget a meeting this morning?"

We both knew I hadn't.

"No." For just a second, he stopped smoothing his moustache, a habit that made me want to hold him down and shave it, and looked the very slightest bit abashed. "Am I keeping you from something?"

I chuckled, although there was no humor in the situation. "Of course not. You know how important you are to this firm and that I am always at your service, Lee. To what do I owe the pleasure?"

There ensued yet another session of going over a minor detail of a corporate acquisition. A detail we'd gone over many times leading to no changes. Then after chewing the subject to an unrecognizable pulp, he set down his cup on my walnut burl coffee table—without benefit of a coaster—and looked me in the eye. "That baby you have? Please start adoption proceedings. We have been, as you know, unable to have children of our own and my relationship needs a boost." He let out a breath and stood, straightening the seam in his bespoke trousers. "And you might as well arrange to transfer him to our care as soon as possible." He left.

I stared into space. Before I allowed my child to become the little boost in that bastard's relationship, I'd see him dead.

The baby wasn't even available for adoption, but Ted seemed to think it wouldn't take long since it had been abandoned. If anyone was going to adopt this baby, it would be me.

Would be us.

But the courts had an alarming viewpoint of homes with married parents and the money to give children everything possible. If we wanted to keep our boy, we needed to look better than Lee. I had a fair nest egg, but compared to him? It would look like a piggy bank.

And if we did what I had in mind, partner or not, I'd be out on my ass, making me an unemployed applicant for adopting that baby.

I picked up the phone and waited for it to ring. "Hey...I think we should get married."

And wasn't that the most romantic proposal ever.

I turned in my notice on the way out, two hours later. Mr. Big City Lawyer was going to be making some very fast changes.

And my omega hadn't even given me an answer yet.

Chapter Twenty-Two

Brandon

What had gotten into my alpha?

"I'm sorry, what did you say?" I was currently holding Brax with one arm and trying like hell to shove a sandwich into my mouth with the other since the babe was truly beyond consolation that morning. Truth be told, I thought he wanted his other papa.

"I said, I think we should get married." His words once again poured hot lava over me in the best way possible. I almost choked on the turkey and cheese. When I failed to answer again, he continued, "Also, I want to adopt Brax, and I've got some things to talk to you about."

"Tonight?" I asked but heard the distinct sounds of Axel getting into his car and shoving the keys into the ignition.

"No, omega mine. Right now. I quit my job. I'm coming home. Be there soon."

He hung up on me then. Axel didn't like talking on the phone while he was driving. I bounced Brax around the house, first because it soothed him, and second because I had to do something to calm down all the nervous energy surging through my veins. Axel quit his job. He wanted to marry me. He wanted to adopt Brax.

Oh, and the other thing, I was pregnant with his babe.

There was a lot of things to pace about, so much so that by the time he got home, my feet ached from the walking up and down the stairs, and my arms ached with a sleeping Brax cradled in them.

"Axel?" I asked as the front door opened.

"Yeah." He came in, and with a smile that spread from one cheek to the other and twinkled in his eyes he kissed me, open mouth, tongue, enough to make every cell in my body flare to life. "Come here, my little man, and you, too, big man. We have to talk."

Maybe he'd changed his mind.

We went to the living room and sat down. I tried to sit a little away from Axel, but he pulled me closer with his free arm. "I would like to explain some things, and please wait until the end before making up your mind."

I nodded since my words and throat were currently not working.

"I told you about that big client, right?" I nodded.

"Well, over drinks and a meeting one night I mentioned Brax. The next thing I know, he's asking about Brax more and more and if he was up for adoption. This morning he was in my office when I arrived. He wants to adopt Brax, and he wanted me to file the paperwork. It's just to appease his mate or something because they can't have kids. That's when it all hit me—like the earth opened and showed me the way. I don't want anyone else to have my family. I don't want Brax to be put to sleep by anyone other than you and me. I don't want anyone making his bottles or rocking him in your chair."

I opened my mouth, but he put his hand up and then kissed my temple.

"When I say I don't want anything to happen to my family, that means you, too. I want you in my life forever, Brandon. I know this all happened with a baby in a box, but it was going to happen eventually. I already liked you, Brandon, maybe even loved you. My job was the only thing holding me back. So I'm laying it all on the table here, love. I want this family. I want us married—two kids—the whole bit."

"And your work?"

He shrugged. "I can always open a small practice here in Roseville. Roseville people need lawyers, too, right?"

I nodded and took one of Brax's toes in my hands while I thought about it.

"Let's do it, then. Let's make this official, and nobody is taking my men. Nobody."

"Do you mean it, omega? You'll be mine?"

I laughed. "Axel, I think I've been yours since the first time you strolled in for a shave. I love you—always have."

"Well, let's do this, then. I'm taking your fine ass to the courthouse. Let's go get Merlin on the way."

"Who is Merlin?" I asked, feeling my face pulled in a grin that just wouldn't stop.

"He's the preacher. I've met him a few times at the club. Let's go."

We raced into action, putting Brax in the car seat and then stopping at Principal Ink. Axel invited everyone to the wedding and Merlin happened to be there, playing pool. We stopped in town for a marriage license, and since my alpha had some connections in the courthouse, they gave it to him right away.

As we drove to city hall, I looked over at his face.

"What?" he asked and then his face lost all its color. "Are you having second thoughts?"

I was. But mostly I was feeling fucking lucky to be

marrying this man and carrying his child.

"Are you marrying me just to keep Brax?" I asked, simply to clear my conscience.

"No. I'm marrying you because I love you—kind of always have, omega."

I nodded as he threaded his fingers through mine.

Inside the courthouse, the guys from Principal Ink had beat us there. In our absence, they had taken seats.

"We don't have rings," I said, swaying back and forth with nausea and nervousness mixed while Brax cooed at people. He was being handed off to Jerry who Brax already loved.

"We don't need rings. I can get them later, love. What matters is this." He put his hand over my heart. "I just need this."

A tear fell down my face. "My heart? You've always had it, Axel."

Chapter Twenty-Three

Axel

Everything changed so fast, my head was still spinning six months later. Turned out Ranger owned another storefront next door to Principal Ink...on the barbershop side, and his tenant had already given notice so it was available almost immediately. I turned in my company car and replaced it with an SUV. The storefront needed quite a bit of work in its change from discount store to nicely appointed law office. Eventually I'd be cashing out certain assets tied into my previous employment, but that might take up to a year, and my city home was still on the market, so these expenses added into the adoption costs and some other things were all coming out of my not-limitless savings. One day I finally hung my shingle outside

Considering I'd put everything I had into becoming a partner in a big-city firm, these changes were good and bad for my sense of self. On the one hand, I'd just thrown out years of long, hard days, blood, sweat, and tears at the drop of a hat. On the other, that hat was my child and nobody was taking him from me. Although my colleagues might feel that walking away from a partnership in the biggest, most prestigious firm in the city was a loss, it took far less time than I thought for me to get past that point and appreciate the pleasures of life in a small town.

I was going over one of the fantastically exciting cases that crossed my desk these days. Unlike at the firm, where I worked on a specific type of contract law, here I handled many kinds of things. This was a will. The elderly lady who hired me had a net worth of almost nothing, but she had sentimental items and a large family, so she wanted to be sure each bit and piece went to the correct relative.

"Ready, alpha?" Brandon stood in the doorway between our places of business, holding Brax in his arms. We had managed to arrange our schedules to keep him with us, but as he was making moves toward mobility, we were going to have to either get more creative or consider daycare. I was voting for creative. "We don't want to keep the judge waiting."

"No, that's never a good idea." I shut the lid on my laptop and stood, stretching. "Let's get this matter resolved while the getting is good."

He grinned and so did the baby. "I promised Brax

ice cream after."

"I thought we agreed no sugar until his birthday cake in a couple of months."

"Okay, he can have strained plums. And we'll have ice cream."

I shook my head and fished my keys from my jeans pocket. One of the best parts of my new practice was the casual attire. Still, I usually wore a little nicer clothes when going to court, but this was not a case where I was the attorney. One of my former partners— without the knowledge of the others who were still angry at my leaving despite the fact my previous client had not paid his bills in quite some time and was not all the fabulousness they'd thought he was. So the eldest founding partner, a man I'd only met a few times, stood beside us in judge's chambers, proudly announcing his intention of being Brax's godfather and making sure "he always had the best of everything."

The judge announced that we were now the official dad and dad of little Brax and cautioned us not to let his godfather spoil him. As if... The guys at Principal Ink were already in charge of that.

Ten minutes later we stood outside the courthouse, me, our son, and my pregnant omega who was going through an ice cream phase and acting as if it was only in celebration. I'd seen his sneaky hoard in the garage freezer, hidden under the bags of frozen veggies.

"So what kind will it be today, omega?" I winked at him. "Maybe something with lots of mix ins?" Somehow, he ate way more than he should in the ice cream department, but the doctor was very happy with his weight and other numbers so I wasn't arguing. He'd lost a lot of weight in the first trimester, hardly able to keep anything down at all, so he had some making up to do, I supposed.

We strolled down the sidewalk toward the new ice cream parlor. His steps slowed as we passed Sugar, but I linked my fingers with his and tugged him past. "Come on, we'll get you a cone but no more or you'll ruin your dinner."

He chuckled. "Have I missed a dinner yet, alpha?"

"No...no you haven't." I tugged him into my body. Brax was asleep in his sling which was not going to be of use once he got just a little bigger. "But it can't be good to eat all sugar all the time."

The breeze was fresh, the sky blue, my omega smiling, and all was right with the world.

Chapter Twenty-Four

Axel

Everything stayed like that, as if we'd earned only good days. Brandon felt well, Brax was proceeding as he should, and we reached the seven-month mark with few blips on the radar. The worst thing that happened was a bad cold from which Brax had had trouble recovering, and since I didn't want my omega catching it, I spent my nights in the nursery with the wheezing little guy and his humidifier/vaporizer for two weeks...then I caught it. So as we crossed off another week on the calendar, reaching eight months, everyone finally well again, and I felt as if I hadn't had my omega alone in an eternity.

Luckily, Ranger had offered to babysit Brax and give us a night to ourselves and I had it all planned.

"I have bigger feet than any hippopotamus, and I can't even see my dick anymore," Brandon groaned, waddling in from the car. He was still cutting hair a couple of nights a week, against my wishes, but as my alpha dad friends told me, there was no stopping an omega when he had something in his mind. So I kept a close eye on him, hoping he'd see the time had come for him to get off those hippo feet and relax a little. "I hate my job."

He flung himself down in the easy chair in the living room, grunting. "Now I'll never be able to get up."

Hmm. Maybe I should have planned this for another night. But I was still willing to try. "Come to the table, omega, and eat. Afterward, I'll give you a nice foot rub." And other things, too, if he was willing.

"Oh...not the table, please, Axel?" His moan was nothing if not dramatic. "Can't we eat in front of the TV? Is the baby asleep?"

Usually he'd have gone and checked on him first thing, and that he didn't had me giving him a second look. "Yes, as always at midnight. You okay?" I cast a regretful look at the table with its flower centerpiece and blew out the candles then prepared TV trays.

"Just tired and sick of being tired and bloated and feeling like I've been pregnant for two hundred years."

I stood the vintage tray in front of him then retrieved the one for me. We'd found them at a yard sale and considered them great treasures. "It's time to stop working until after the baby comes, omega," I told him, settling on the couch and lifting my knife and fork. I paused, noticing he was staring at the plate. "Don't you like it?"

"What is it?" He poked at it with a finger, curling his upper lip. Uh-oh.

"Chicken Prince Orloff." I'd slaved over it.

"Do I eat that?"

"Yes, you love it." I cut a piece of mine and held it to his lips. "Come on, take a taste."

He cast me the fish eye, but obediently opened his mouth and closed it over the morsel. He chewed. I waited. "Not bad," he admitted grudgingly. "Chicken...what ham and cheese and stuff."

"And stuff," I agreed, feeling less sympathetic and more irritated that I'd planned a feast and seduction for a man who really wanted ice cream and a nap. Then I reminded myself it wasn't his fault that he felt awful. Then I felt guilty.

"Frozen from Costco?"

Ohhh, guilty all gone. "No," I bit out. "I spent four hours making it."

"Is there dessert?"

Hormones. Pregnancy hormones were making my omega a little jerky. He didn't feel well...and I had to keep my cool.

"Yes, omega," I said, trying for an even tone. "I

made a triple layer chocolate cake with raspberry coulis." And before he could ask, "And bought some premium vanilla ice cream from the shop for on top."

He paused with the fork halfway to his lips and smiled. "You did all this for me?" Hormones went both ways. Tears spilled down his cheeks. "I am the luckiest omega in the world to have someone like you. Can I ask you something, alpha?"

I nodded, wary but hopeful.

"Would you mind awfully making love to me before dessert? I feel like that's been a long time, too."

My heart split in two and I stood and gathered him in my arms. "Mind, omega?" My voice was harsh, and I hardly recognized it. "There is nothing I'd love more." He was heavier, but not heavy enough for me not to be able to carry him to our bed where I laid him down and slowly undressed him. His belly jutted high, filled with our child, almost ready to be born and join his brother in the nursery and in our lives.

When he was naked, I knelt on the bed and caressed his body, wanting to bring every inch of skin to life before taking things any further. I followed my palms with my lips, kissing and nibbling until I reached his cock, which was standing straight up and ready for me. "Omega, you may not be able to see this, right now, but you're missing out." I took a long lick down one side and up the other. "Yes, this is one fine cock." I blew a stream of cool air over it and sat back on my heels.

"Alpha, please," he moaned. "Don't toy with me. I'm not in any shape for it."

I trailed a finger over the swollen head, smearing the drop of precum. "Mmm. So what would you have me do, then?"

"Please take me into your mouth and suck me. Before I just explode anyway."

"Your wish is my command." And my joy. I still sucked on just the head for a minute or two, but then I took him to the back of my throat and sucked hard. If I did this right the ice cream and cake would have to wait until morning.

Chapter Twenty-Five

Brandon

Brax, Axel, and I were having lunch. I'd packed up a picnic, but since he was busy, we settled for eating in his office at the tiny round table. It was amazing how many clients had sprung up in Roseville. Axel's apartment in the city had sold at last, and now he was home every night, just like we liked it.

We'd had a small birthday party for Brax. He had his first cake and ice cream and enjoyed every second of it. Axel even hired a professional photographer to come in and take pics of the birthday party and then me afterward in all my whale-ish glory.

But he didn't complain about my new figure. In fact, my alpha seemed to love it.

"You have to work tonight?" Axel asked, frowning.

"I do. It's my last night for the rest of the pregnancy. I'm glad, to be honest. I keep bumping into things with my belly."

He squinted. "I'm not sure I like you humping into people—especially those guys down there at the shop."

I cracked up and nearly choked on my sandwich.

"I didn't say humping, I said bumping. There's a difference."

He smiled. I knew that smile. He was screwing with me. "I know. But still. I'm glad it's the last night. I kind of like all my boys home at night."

Truth be told, I'd considered leaving the shop after I had the baby. I would have a one-year-old and a newborn and that thought in itself almost threw me into a tizzy.

"We like our alpha home, don't we?" I rubbed my belly, and he took a turn after me.

"Okay, lunchtime over. Let's let Daddy get back to work." I stood and had begun to gather the food with Axel's help when an almost cramp took over my lower belly, and before I could react, a sploosh of water was at my feet.

"Oh, so that's what that feels like." I looked at Axel, and his face had lost all its color.

"Let's get to the doctor. Your bag is in your car, right?"

"Oh, um, yeah. What about Brax?"

Axel moved into action but didn't seem the least bit nervous. I loved that about him, his cool under pressure.

"We can drop him off with Ranger. He will take

care of him."

I nodded, and we rushed to the car. A pain, deep and seething, took over my back, and I stopped to grab Axel's biceps. "Let's hurry, mate. I think this babe is in a rush to be with us."

We dropped off Brax with the bag that I had packed for him. We knew one of the guys would be taking care of him, but didn't know which one. It didn't matter. Any of them would take care of our babe just as well as we would.

By the time we got to the hospital, my contractions were a minute or less apart. They weren't screaming painful, but I had gritted my teeth more than once, trying not to scream and scare the crap out of Axel while he drove.

"We need to get into a room, now!" Axel ground out using his attorney voice, which he had also used a few times in the bedroom.

The nurses put me in a room and checked to make sure I was dilating. When one of them came up from the sheet with wide eyes, I knew it was time.

"Let me get the doctor. This babe is ready to come out—now."

My body urged with the need to bear down. "Axel, get down there. I don't think the doctor is going to make it."

"You want me to..." He nodded and went to the end of the bed. I bent my knees and bore down once and felt the ring of fire I'd read about.

"Oh gods, there's the head. Come on, doctor!" he screamed, but I knew better. One more push, and our babe was out.

"It's a girl. It's a beautiful girl." He held our babe in his arms right at the moment the doctor came in flanked by two nurses. They took our girl from Axel and helped me with the afterbirth. Axel was so torn. I saw it in his face. His gaze bobbed from me to the babe and back again. I winked at him in an attempt to let him know it was okay.

Our girl screamed from the time she came out until she was back in her daddy's arms again, clean and with her cord cut. While they cleaned her up, my sheets were changed and, in thirty minutes, it was as though we'd had her all along.

"She's gorgeous," I cooed as Axel laid her on my chest.

"What's her name?" he asked me.

"We loved Ruthie, right?"

He murmured, "Brax and Ruthie. Sounds just about right for my family."

It hit me then that in those ten months since our little Brax had arrived in the most unplanned way, that we had become a family. The man that I'd always longed for was now my husband and the father of my two children. It wasn't the way I would choose for Brax's sake, but it turned out for the best.

"I love our family and you," I said, heart bursting with love.

"I love you and our babes more than life, omega mine."

Epilogue

Brandon

"I need water, please," I whined at Axel. Ruthie was in a growth spurt and nursing so much that I felt like I was a desert.

"Here, I already anticipated," Axel said, bringing another huge cup of ice water to the side of the bed and kissing Ruthie's head as she nursed.

"You're the best."

He popped the waistband of his pajama pants with a grin. "Yep. I am."

Lying next to us, he flicked through some paperwork while I caught up on my newest Netflix addiction.

Ruthie fell asleep, milk wasted, and I maneuvered her to the crib in the next room right beside Brax's crib. She was now sleeping through the night.

I showered quickly and got into bed, completely exhausted. "I need sleep," I groaned into my pillow.

"How about a vacation?" Axel asked me, rubbing my back.

"A vacation sounds amazing, but you just started

your practice." I'd quit my job shortly after having Ruthie. I never thought I'd be a stay-at-home dad, but it simply made sense, given our situation.

"Well, that's good because we leave tomorrow. I already packed your stuff."

I raised up to make sure he wasn't lying. "You're serious?"

He nodded. "I am. I'm bringing my family to the mountains. I rented a cabin far away from everyone. Just the four of us, clean air, and quiet."

I rolled to lay my head in his lap. "Thank you for being you."

He laughed. "Thank you for giving me everything. I should've fessed up about being a lawyer months before I did."

I shrugged. "But then we wouldn't have Brax. It all happened for a reason, Axel. I wouldn't change any of it."

His face grew serious. "So, you trust me now? Have I earned that back?"

I straddled his legs. "Of course you have. Were you really worried about that?"

My mate nodded. "I was. You can't have a good marriage or family without trust."

I kissed his lips, softly at first, and then he opened

his mouth for me. "You have my trust, my love, my heart, and my soul."

He chuckled and pulled my hips closer. "Then I have everything, omega."

An Excerpt from The Alpha's Principal-Kissed Omega

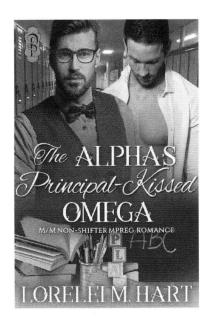

Chapter One

Henry Coastal

A first day in a new school was always nerve-racking. And a first day in a new school in a new town where I knew almost nobody? Enough to send me into a tailspin. But after the breakup, I just couldn't face seeing him…either of them…every day at work.

So, I put feelers out and was lucky enough to find a position mid-year, which I snapped up. The fact my new job was in a small town had actually been a negative, but one I was willing to look past. Parking my car in the faculty lot, I turned off the key and sat for a moment, looking at the red-brick building. No fence surrounded it, and the doors were propped open to catch the spring breeze. The windows were also open, and ivy crept halfway up the walls to curl around the decorative elements in the brickwork. Quite charming, and after the inner-city campus, where faculty had to use a thumbprint to enter, and students went through a metal detector, quite head-spinning.

I knew nothing about the teacher I was replacing except that his pregnancy had become high-risk, and his doctor ordered him into bed for the duration. I would be teaching a variety of classes, including world history, political science, and geography. And omega studies. That should prove interesting. I'd actually requested a woman teach that, but no one was available, and the principal, a Mr. Armison with twinkling eyes, a stern jaw, and immaculate white shirt with sleeves rolled up to show forearms that made me drool, patted me on the back, told me he had faith in me and not to be sexist, and ushered me out of his office.

I wanted to explain that it wasn't sexism, but that I hadn't taught it before and worried about having enough time to get it right, but somehow hadn't found the words before the brown-and-beige diamond-shaped floor tiles of the hallway were under my feet.

If I hadn't been so focused on his looks and his scent of sandalwood and some obscure spice, I might have been more effective in my campaign. But I would make it work. I'd make it all work.

The last day of spring break, a Monday in this district, meant no students would be around, making the wide-open school even more unusual, but it was warm for March, and perhaps the maintenance staff sought to air out the building while they could. I piled my rolling cart high and started for the nearest door, making lists in my mind of everything I sought to accomplish before I faced my students on Tuesday morning.

I had been less than impressed with the classroom decor, although the lack of graffiti indoors and out was refreshing. In the city I'd had to work hard to create an inviting atmosphere for students who made their complete lack of interest in attending clear. I'd gone home every day exhausted and returned to throw all my energy into trying to make a dent in their armor. My ex never felt that way, convinced his job was to show up, offer knowledge, and if those he offered it to didn't want to learn English, their loss.

So my tears and exhaustion were a constant source of conflict between us.

Add in my desire to marry and start a family, something he claimed he was not ready for yet—as evidenced by a brief affair with the school basketball coach—and we were doomed. I'd spent the last two weeks couch hopping to avoid going home. And this weekend moving everything into storage. Technically, I was homeless, staying at a budget motel outside of town until I found a place to rent.

But my classroom would always be home to me, and I hoped to the kids I taught. So, instead of hunting for an apartment, I would spend today preparing my room for the students. While my contract was technically that of a long-term sub, I was in no position to complain. I'd find something permanent before the fall, I hoped.

Entering the school, I once again took in the clean, neat interior with its many displays of student artwork and awards. I would not likely be able to stay here past the spring term, since it was not a big institution and when the omega returned from paternity leave in the fall, they wouldn't have room for me. But I'd enjoy it while I could.

"Mr. Coastal, there you are!" The source of my daydreams strode down the hallway toward me, just as I was about to open my—also not locked—classroom door. "I wanted to make sure you had everything you need."

Need yes, want? I could think of a few things. "I need to go through the cupboards, but as long as the students all have their textbooks, I have Mr. Crimson's lesson plans." I paused. "Am I expected to follow them to the letter?"

"No, but if you stray too far, make sure you cover the state requirements for each level. You are probably familiar with them from your previous school, correct."

"Yes, sir, but I like to do a lot of extra projects and try to bring history and the other subjects to life as much as possible. I want the kids to know how to be citizens ready to participate when they graduate, and I find the curriculum is often lacking in those areas."

He grinned, and my blood pressure rose by at least twenty points. Always handsome, smiling, he was supermodel handsome. On this student-free day, he was dressed more casually, in a fitted polo shirt and jeans that left little to the imagination. As in, they clung to powerful thighs I wanted to bite. "We expect our faculty to share their passions in their field of study wherever possible. It's one of the keys to success we believe. Looks like you'll fit right in."

He clapped me on the back and turned to walk away then stopped. "Oh, before I forget, we need your permanent address for the files. I know you just moved to town."

Oh man. "I umm...I haven't found a place yet, since I moved so suddenly." *Damn, don't say it that way. He'll ask questions you may not want to answer!* "I thought I'd check online listings this evening."

"I see." Now he hesitated. "I don't know what you have in mind, but I have a father-in-law's apartment over the garage I usually rent out. The teacher you are replacing lived there before he married his alpha, in fact."

Chapter Two

Ranger Armison

Refreshing was the word I would use to describe a teacher like Henry. I could see on his desk myriad lists and lesson plans along with his laptop, playing some kind of instrumental piano music. He was a committed teacher, and our school could use more of those.

Though on the surface, he seemed quite the opposite of me, I knew there was a connection and I wanted to explore it further.

Way further.

When he said he didn't have a place to live, my instincts kicked into gear. My alpha instincts.

"I don't know what you have in mind, but I have a father-in-law's apartment over the garage. I usually rent it out. The teacher you are replacing lived there before he married his alpha, in fact."

Henry's eyes widened and he nodded almost too eagerly. Oh, the omega had no idea how much his eagerness turned me on.

"If that would be all right, I would love to move in." He cleared his throat as though he'd said something wrong. "I mean, thank you. Would you mind if I move in tonight? I've been couch surfing and motel sleeping for far too long."

I took in his appearance. He was the typical teacher fantasy wrapped all up in a gorgeous package. His glasses, thick and black propped at the top of his nose did a good job of trying to hide his gorgeous two-toned eyes. One was green while the other was a pale brown. His full lips made the most of accentuating his firm jawline and cleft chin.

A cleft chin was a sign of great intelligence, or so I'd been told.

He filled out his gray slacks in all the right places, and the V-neck sweater did things to this principal, things that should be handled in my office, over my knee, with my hand.

And Henry calling out my name.

"Mr Armison?" he asked and I realized I'd been in Henry-sexville in my mind. I cleared my throat and turned, trying to hide the raging boner I had already, just at the thought of him naked.

"Of course. In fact, here's the key and I will text you the address." I wrestled with the metal ring and finally got the key to the garage apartment untangled from it. "I will see you tomorrow, Henry."

"Not tonight?" he asked and I gasped. Did he want to see me already?

"Tonight?" I inquired, looking at him over my shoulder because still raging boner.

"I meant when I move in."

I shuffled on my feet. "I also own a business, and I have to work tonight. I get in pretty late. But I will see you tomorrow. Good luck. I have a feeling this school will be better because of your presence."

And with that, I left the room before I kissed him senseless and then bent him over the desk for a proper lesson.

Get a grip, Ranger. He's probably not even interested.

With all of my school tasks completed, I walked out to the parking lot and, while walking across the parking lot, noticed Henry getting into a beat-up car that probably belonged in the junkyard. He saw me and waved, and I did the same before putting my backpack on both shoulders. I waited until he left, strolling slowly through the lot. I had to lock up after he left.

Henry was watching me, the sexy little devil.

Then again, I was watching him as well.

After he finally drove out, I got onto my

161

motorcycle after strapping on my helmet.

I revved up the cycle and took off, eager to get done with my second job and get home. I drove the three or four miles to my shop and parked my bike right under the awning that read Principal Ink. With my bike right in front of the window where I would be working for the night, I could keep an eye on it.

"Afternoon, boss man," Mike said from behind the counter. "You have appointments lined up for the entire night. Ever since you showed that portrait on social media, they have been calling in."

"The whole night?" I asked, excited about the business, but also a little bummed I wouldn't be able to see Henry again that night.

"Yep. Your last appointment is at midnight, and it's a big one." He showed me a picture of an intricate dahlia along with a skull. It would take me hours. "Your first client is already here."

I looked over to see a young man bouncing his knee. I got that a lot, first time nervousness.

"Give me five minutes to set up," I said to anyone who was listening and went to my station. I took off the button-down and tie of my day job to reveal a T-shirt with my logo on it. Mike had already sterilized and set up my tools, so I looked over to the young man and said, "Come on. Let's get this started."

I finished up my appointment about two in the morning and barely dragged myself home. I looked up from the driveway to see Henry's car parked in my usual spot and one soft light on inside the upstairs apartment.

He was here, in my place.

And I kind of liked seeing his car in my space— didn't mind it at all.

After showering off the events of the day and getting into bed, I let my mind wander, half-asleep, to Henry.

I reached down, under the covers, to grip my cock and picture my new teacher omega doing all the things I wanted him to, but sleep had other plans. But with his image in my mind, I rolled over and fell into a deep sleep.

About the Authors

Lorelei M. Hart is the cowriting team of USA Today Bestselling Authors Kate Richards and Ever Coming as well as Ophelia Heart, another bestselling author. Friends for years, the trio decided to come together and write one of their favorite guilty pleasures: Mpreg. There is something that just does it for them about smexy men who love each other enough to start a family together in a world where they can do it the old-fashioned way.

Sign up for our Newsletter.
Check out the Shifters of Distance
Lorelei's Amazon Page